CAVE-IN

Great Plains Publications gratefully acknowledges the financial support provided for
its publishing program by the Government of Canada through the Canada Book
Fund; the Canada Council for the Arts; the Province of Manitoba through the Book
Publishing Tax Credit and the Book Publisher Marketing Assistance Program; and the
Manitoba Arts Council.

Design & Typography by Relish New Brand Experience
Printed in Canada by Friesens

Library and Archives Canada Cataloguing in Publication

Title: Cave-in / Pam Withers.
Names: Withers, Pam, author.
Identifiers: Canadiana (print) 20240386310 | Canadiana (ebook) 20240400410 |
    ISBN 9781773371245 (softcover) | ISBN 9781773371252 (EPUB)
Subjects: LCGFT: Action and adventure fiction. | LCGFT: Novels.
Classification: LCC PS8595.I8453 C38 2024 | DDC jC813/.54—dc23

ENVIRONMENTAL BENEFITS STATEMENT

Great Plains Press saved the following resources by
printing the pages of this book on chlorine free paper
made with 100% post-consumer waste.

TREES	WATER	ENERGY	SOLID WASTE	GREENHOUSE GASES
11	880	5	37	4,740
FULLY GROWN	GALLONS	MILLION BTUs	POUNDS	POUNDS

Environmental impact estimates were made using the Environmental Paper Network
Paper Calculator 4.0. For more information visit www.papercalculator.org

Canadä

FSC
www.fsc.org

MIX

Paper | Supporting
responsible forestry

FSC® C016245

CAVE-IN

PAM WITHERS

yellow dog

Dedicated to Jane Ghieuw and Michelle James, with love.
And hugs to Theo Nakitsas Wardlaw.

"Follow humbly wherever and to whatever abysses nature leads, or you shall learn nothing."
—*Thomas Huxley, biologist*

CHAPTER ONE

It's dark as tar ahead, and my hands and knees throb from a long crawl through a short entrance tunnel. As the cave ceiling lowers, I drop to the ground and wriggle onward, gloved hands thrust forward like a swimmer doing the breaststroke. Jagged rocks scrape my elbows as my headlamp searches the inky blackness. The sound of huffing behind me reassures me that my new caving partner Jett is keeping up.

"Hudson?" comes Jett's muffled voice.

"Yeah?"

"I'm frickin' stuck. Like, stuck solid." There's a flutter of panic in his tone.

Directing a calm voice under my lifted armpit, I say, "No, you're not. You're temporarily detained."

"Seriously, I can't move forward. Need to try and back out."

"Shouldn't've eaten that chocolate bar. Just hold still and do deep breaths." Given that panicked newbies can get an adrenalin surge that temporarily swells their body, I figure Jett just needs to calm himself.

"Huds! I'm telling you, I can't move."

"Chill, Jett. Want me to squirt you with dish soap and pull?" An actual technique but used only in serious rescues.

"Very funny."

"I'm feeling cool air on my face," I tell Jett. "And I hear flowing water ahead. That means this cave keeps going."

"I'm unstuck now," Jett announces.

"Of course you are, genius." I wriggle farther forward, negotiating an elbow-shaped bend by rolling my body onto its side, like a luge sledder taking a tight turn. "A crazy python designed this," I mutter.

"And who's following the crazy python?" asks Jett.

"We are. Cave prodigies at sixteen, remember?" Actual words used to describe my former caving partner and me when we got written up in the school paper last year. So that's Jett now, too, I told him. It's what Jett wants: to improve till he feels part of Tass's high school caving crowd, even if the five of us are fractured into two cliques now, something Jett doesn't like.

"You mean it's not all about mapmaking?" Jett teases, sounding like my dad, who started me caving at age four and whose caving *is* all about mapmaking.

"That too."

Minutes later, the tunnel having expanded to a comfy, hunched-walk height, the whiff of air I've been following turns into a gust that I gulp greedily. Now that I'm more relaxed, I feel a tinge of guilt that there are only two of us on this caving venture. There's a caving code called Rule of Three. *One to stay behind if someone is injured while another goes for help.* Yeah, Dad should be with us this morning, but he wasn't available, and we had this new entrance calling to us, like really urging us to make a new discovery, and we're hot stuff, so rules are meant to be broken sometimes, right?

"Yes!" I shout as my headlamp illuminates a pizza-size hole in an otherwise dead-end rock wall of this deep cavern. A small pizza, unfortunately. I squeeze my head and headlamp-mounted helmet through the gap and lower my chin to aim the beam downward. *Way* down. We're talking a serious drop-off.

Shivering with excitement, I watch the feeble glow reveal a huge body of water, perhaps the size of an Olympic swimming pool. Then I lift my eyes to a soaring, stalactite-studded ceiling, and a dim wall in the distance. The water is hemmed in on all sides by steep, glistening limestone walls. It's like a four-storey-tall solarium minus pool-decking and lighting—and we are for sure the first humans to see it. Take that, Mica! Wait till my former caving partner hears about this.

On the far side, a tinkling sound indicates a stream running into it—which means a potential passage beyond, if only we could squirt safely through the pizza hole, splash into the pool, and swim across it.

"What?" Jett demands, tapping my back. "You're blocking the hole."

With cold air blasting past my ears, I pull my head back through, too stunned to declare what I've just seen. Aladdin, Alice, Indiana Jones, and Gollum—they'd all be so jealous.

"Serious booty," I whisper, using the caving word for a virgin cave. "Big chamber full of water. Super amazing."

Jett's eyes widen, and he elbows his way over to the window. Given his head is bigger than mine, he removes his helmet and stuffs his flashlight into his mouth to stick his face through the opening. It's such a tight squeeze that I worry he'll get stuck like that and create a swim-hall gargoyle frightening any bats on the other side.

"Holy," Jett says softly as he pulls his head back into our space. He slaps me on the back. "We're going to be so famous, Huds!"

Funny he says "we," since I don't think Jett cares a crap about fame, just about improving as a caver and hanging out with me. But he knows how much *I* crave it. I see no reason to pretend otherwise.

I smile. Yes, we are going to be famous. Even if it took a while to convince Jett to up his caving game six months ago when Mica and I fell apart.

There's silence but for the drip-drip of the cave, the slap of Jett putting his helmet back on his head, and the anxious tapping of my boot.

"It's *huge!*" Jett says. "The biggest find in Tass ever!"

Tass is the pockmarked, cave-rich town we live in here on northern Vancouver Island, Canada. Population three hundred.

"There are going to be scientists and reporters all over us!" he predicts, which again I suspect is for my benefit. Is my craving for fame so obvious?

"No there aren't," I correct him. "Especially since we're not telling anyone unless that secret Door is the other side of this new chamber." The possibility makes my skin prickle. *The Door* is what we've named the passage we're trying to find that connects Tass's western cave system with the eastern one. Or, as we call them, the Castle and the Dungeon.

"The secret Door is probably a crack we'll never fit through," Jett says, "or more likely there's no connection at all. And even if we find it, who's really going to care but Mica and his buddies, who might discover it first anyway? Or maybe the two of you will get over your little argument and be caving together again by then."

"Way more than a little argument, Jett, and stop sounding like my dad." Then I drop my voice to really mimic my father: "It's highly unlikely the two systems connect, and you're going to get yourself hurt if you keep obsessing about it. Exploring caves is about fun and mapmaking."

Jett and I both chuckle. I picture our den at home, full of pencilled maps, the best ones locked in a safe. Someday Dad, Jett, and I will join them all into one, producing the first underground map of the whole Tass region. We'll get Parks Canada to open the caves to the public, creating a big tourist destination and jobs for ourselves running cave tours. That'd be way better than gutting fish at the local fish plant after high school. Mica and his new caving partners will do anything for a chance to cave with us after that. Till then, though, the maps remain top secret.

"I'm naming it Pool Dome," I declare. That's my favourite part of being a cave explorer, naming what I discover.

"Can you believe how high the ceiling is?" Jett says. "Must be really close to the surface. What's over us, anyway?"

"We're just north of town," I guess. The ceiling is so high it must be barely supporting some section outside Tass. We're somewhere near the logging company's operation centre, where Dad drives and Mom's a bookkeeper.

"Could be under the machinery depot," Jett says. "The new parking lot where they've been putting logging trucks and bull-dozers between shifts."

"They took down a lot of trees to build that parking lot," I say. "Now there aren't enough tree roots to hold back water. Plus, they built the road that leads to the lot, kind of close to a stream. Hope that doesn't mess with the stream's water flow. Hey, know how much a logging truck weighs?"

"No," Jett says impatiently.

"Same as three elephants."

"Wow. Have they tested the stability in that parking lot, given that Tass is full of sinkholes?" Jett asks.

Before I can respond, an eerie vibration flows through the cave. Did I imagine it? Jett's gloved hands touch the wall, like he felt it too.

We raise our eyes to the nubby ceiling of the cul-de-sac and back away from the window. I leap back to stare into the pool cavern. Body taut, I listen to a low rumble coming from its rafters, high above the pool, a menacing growl. My headlamp picks out dust sifting down, my nostrils flare in response to an earthy—earthier—smell, while my boots pick up an accelerated trembling.

"Get out, *now!*" Jett shouts, lunging for me.

CHAPTER TWO

Despite Jett's efforts, I'm under some kind of spell, glued to the window over the new chamber.

Jett's shouting, "Hudson! Hudson!" as he pulls me away, but it all sounds far away and feels like slow-motion.

A roar like a dynamite blast deafens me. I begin to shake. The dome over the swimming pool cracks and disintegrates like an eggshell. Meteor-size rocks thunder into the water, creating explosive waves half lit by patches of filthy new daylight. The splashes reach icy fingers up the walls and through the viewing hole. They slap me in the face as I'm tugged backwards with a drowned-out scream. Jett feeds me into the shuddering tunnel behind us. I'm suddenly okay with the way he's punching my ass to speed me up toward the way we came in. The two of us are high-speed belly-crawling, then half-rising, stooping, elbowing, racing through the tunnel like spooked rats. A blast of air from the collapse chases us up the passage.

When I feel daddy longlegs on my neck, my pounding heart slows. They're not poisonous and exist only a short distance from daylight.

Finally, we're bursting out of the cavity we discovered only yesterday, a new mini sinkhole that's a ten-minute stroll from my backyard. Damp grass never smelled so sweet. Daylight never felt so good, so bright, so warm. It's June, it smells like spring, and school will be done for the year very shortly. *School out.* I need to think of that or *anything* other than what just happened. But now we're instantly jarred by the deafening bongs of an iron bell. The bell tower on Tass's firehall serves as a town-rousing emergency system, for forest fires, earthquakes, hurricanes, landslides, sinkholes, etc. I cover my ears and join Jett stumbling down the hill, then across our un-mowed grass.

"Earthquake or over-heavy logging trucks breaking through the cave ceiling?" Jett's voice cracks.

"Don't know, but let's find out," I say, voice hoarse. If it's an earthquake, we've been lucky to escape. Even as I struggle to slow my pulse, I realize that had I stayed where I was just a second longer, or if our pizza window had been larger, I could've been injured or killed. Jett saved me. His instincts are good. My regard for him as a caving partner rises.

I breathe in deeply, then breathe out. How lucky am I to live where forest meets sea, and fresh air, soil, and water mix the way nature intended? Beneath our sleepy town lie air pockets between layers of limestone—layers upon layers of secret chambers with jewelled ceilings that only cavers can find, understand, or appreciate. Someday the world will line up to stare in awe at these wonders. I will be one of the guides who opens their eyes to the magic of caves.

But what of the prize chamber we just discovered? Fully collapsed, pulverized, filled with unstable rubble? An unknown masterpiece, destroyed?

"What causes sinkholes?" Jett asks.

"Water," I reply. "It washes soil away between rocks underground, which makes cavities the surface eventually sags into. Then the water in those gaps freezes and thaws, making them less stable."

"So, it's just nature doing its thing?" he asks as we near my house.

"Can be. Or it can be unnatural, like when too many trees are chopped down near a stream."

"Hudson! Jett!" my mother is screaming over the bell clangs. Ignoring our filthy state, she and my dad sprint across the yard and clasp both of us at once, tears falling onto the collar of her dress.

"You okay?" Dad asks, gripping my shoulders.

"I'm fine. Where are you going?" I call out as Jett veers left just feet from our back door. His hands are over his ears, trying to block out the clanging bell.

"Home before my parents freak," he shouts back. His face is the colour of ash.

"What's with the emergency bell?" I ask my parents, lifting my hands to cover my ears.

"There's been a cave-in," Dad says, turning his eyes uphill.

"How bad?"

"I don't know."

"Then let's go find out."

We head toward Main Street's turnoff to the logging yard, joined by a swarm of other citizens. We find ourselves following two firetrucks, lights flashing, headed up the hill.

Striding well ahead of my parents, I manage to manoeuvre myself just feet away from a certain new classmate, Ana. She's the sixteen-year-old daughter of a new family in town, the Toops. Mr. Toop is VP of Tass Tree Felling, otherwise known as TTF, or more commonly around here, just TT. Ana's blond hair is fanned out in the spring breeze, and she's wearing a red track suit and sturdy white hi-tops. She's marching so fast it's an effort to draw up beside her.

"Hey Ana," I say, breathing hard. I move slightly uphill so she'll think I'm taller than I am. "What's happened?"

It's only the second time I've met her, and she's dangerously good-looking, as most of the guys at school have already noted. More important, she's rumoured to be a caver.

"A sinkhole, someone said." Her jade eyes are fixed on the trucks' flashing lights ahead. "I heard you get them a lot here, but this must be a really big one. An emergency? Hope no one fell in. Or was caving at the time," she adds pointedly, looking my clothes up and down. "You could maybe lose the helmet now."

Heat rushing to my face, I unstrap my caving helmet and buckle it onto my pack's strap.

"At least it's Sunday. Maybe no one was up there," I say hesitantly.

"Up where?" she asks, turning and locking her eyes on mine. An electric current travels up my spine.

"The new machinery depot. Logging yard. Where they park the big trucks and machines. I think maybe one got swallowed by a new sinkhole." If I'm trying to impress her, there's no sign it's working.

"And you know this because?" Her pretty eyes have narrowed.

We're now in sight of halted emergency vehicles, and we hustle closer to glimpse an emergency crew placing yellow tape around the edges of a new crater half the size of a soccer field. A red backhoe is teetering on the edge of the collapsed surface, like something poised to dive, prevented from doing so only by strands of tangled tree roots. It looks determined to join the giant dump truck that's up to its windshield in rubble and muddy water maybe four storeys below. My heart sinks. I'm looking at the exposed innards, the very sad remains, of my newly christened Pool Dome.

"Were you there, underground, when it happened, Hudson Greer? Did you do something to set it off? My dad says there are saboteurs around here, eco-dickheads who are against logging or something." Her hands are on her hips, elbows bent, and she's studying me, eyes large and wary.

"What? You're accusing me? Both my parents work for your dad, Ana! And the last thing this town needs is a sinkhole disaster! If you're a caver—are you? You know no caver would deliberately—"

"Sorry," she says, shoving her pink-manicured hands into her tracksuit trouser pockets. "You just seemed to know—And you've obviously just come from—Sorry, that was a very rude thing to say. The shock of such a big disaster right here in Tass is messing with my mind. It's terrible, isn't it? I'm glad you didn't get hurt."

"Yeah, I hope no one got hurt." We both go silent, surveying the giant hole.

"You are kind of a caving maniac, though, aren't you?" she asks. "So I hear. A BNC around here."

One of her eyebrows rises as those green eyes scan me again. BNC stands for big-name caver. My chest expands and heart ascends.

"Some people think all cavers are maniacs."

She laughs lightly, grabs a rubber band from her coat pocket, and pulls her hair into a ponytail. "Yes, I've done caving. But Dad says over his dead body here in Tass. He thinks it's too dangerous because of all the sinkholes. So, I guess I'm an ex-caver now. And this, this emergency today, sure isn't going to change that."

"It's bad," I acknowledge. "But welcome to Tass, Ana, and hope you like it here."

"Seriously? Like there's anything to do in this place."

She has a point. Tass, British Columbia, famous for nothing but logging, a closed-down mine, ominous sinkholes, and half a dozen boring caves open to tourists along with dozens that are not. It's accessible only by a gravel road from Strathcona Provincial Park, a chunk of wild backcountry nearly the size of Yosemite National Park, with bears, cougars, and all. "World famous caving district," a sign into town announces. Another jokes, "Population: more or less."

"Ana!" a loud male voice calls. Her father.

Before I can point out things we—er, she—can do in tame but interesting Tass, she whirls around and beelines to a bunch of important-looking logging boss-types wearing bright orange safety vests. There are four of them, and they're huddled on a tongue of turf sticking out into the giant new sinkhole. Is where they're standing even safe? She halts beside her hard-hatted dad. He's in deep conversation with the mayor. Of course.

"Hudson." The deep voice comes from my left elbow.

"Oh, hi, Mr. Williams." My science teacher.

"It's a major one, eh? But no one was killed or injured. Still, TT is going to take an economic hit, which is bad for Tass. Maybe they'll pay more attention to safety. Get some inspectors in."

"Inspectors cost money," I say.

"Inspectors help keep the area environmentally compliant. Which might also prevent some sinkholes," Mr. Williams says. "Would love a student or two to get involved in environmental activism around here."

He pats me on my shoulder. I frown. *Does he mean me?* I'm no environmental lobbyist, just a kid who caves.

"Well, *I* like the idea of inspectors visiting Tass," says Dad, appearing behind us. "Maybe our caving maps would help them find potential trouble spots."

"No!" I object.

"Always the optimist, honey." Mom sighs from beside him. "You're talking about amateur, hand-drawn maps versus politicians and business interests, you know."

"Science and the truth win out every time, dear." Dad gives Mom a peck on the cheek and me a pat on the shoulder. "I'm off to check on my vehicles and maybe have a word with Mr. Toop and Lucas."

Lucas is Mayor Brown—also Mica's dad. He has just appeared on that dicey lookout with the other boss-types. Dad and he went to school together, even used to cave together, though nowadays they seem to avoid each other more often than they chat. When I ask him if something went down between them, he always shrugs and says "Just one of those things. Ancient history."

"Those officials need to be careful," I say, eyeing the edges of the crater. It's a sinkhole, one of many that infest our community. But this one is not just way bigger and closer to town, it's a tragic new grave: the buried remains of the most beautiful chamber ever. One Jett and I had been the first and last to see. I slink away from Mom and Mr. Williams to stand closer to the disaster zone.

CHAPTER THREE

"Toothpick, look at you in your caving grots. Always showing up overdressed for the occasion."

My stomach hardens at the sarcastic voice referring to my size and worn, torn, dirt-caked jeans and sweatshirt. Not to mention the caving helmet strapped on my backpack. I feel my shoulders slump a little. Slowly, I lift my chin and force myself to look at Mica.

"Were you actually caving during that cave-in? Bet that scared the crap out of you. You are so lucky to be alive, I'm thinking."

"Hi, Mica," I say stiffly.

"Looks like we've got a new entrance to the underworld." He jerks his head toward the sinkhole. "For those who dare."

"Help yourself, Mica. I only team up with people I can trust."

"Oooh, someone's in a mood," Mica says in his nasally voice. It's a voice I used to listen to, even respect. I miss the person he was. We had each other's backs, were proud of our skills, and shared a sense of adventure like no one else. Until it all went wrong. "Well," he says, "at least no one was hurt this time. Not like in the Big One."

In Tass, the "Big One" is town legend. It happened before Mica and I were born and before Mom moved to Tass, but Dad was a teenager and lost his father in it. Mica's great-grandfather died in the same disaster. The church, steeple and all, disappeared when the ground beneath it opened up with no warning, swallowing the entire building and its congregation. There was a Search and Rescue team, people willing to risk their lives trying to locate mangled bodies. But they eventually gave up; no remains were ever found. It was that deep and that dangerous. Rumoured to be seven storeys down. The crater was eventually filled, and a memorial garden was installed on the disappeared church's plot. Some people say that on a still night, you can hear the faint sound of a choir singing hymns there. Jett and I, we'd never go caving under it. Though I'd probably be tempted if Dad weren't so adamant about "respecting the dead." He probably has awful memories from losing his father that way.

"Remind your dad this could have been another Big One if it had been a workday," I say bitterly, watching the bosses and Ana, now hard-hatted, peer into the pit. Mica is as full of himself as his father since his dad was elected mayor last December. Weeks later, the caving accident that split up our partnership only made things worse. He seems to get off on being the high school's power-monger. He has minions like he's some kind of mob boss. If Mica targets someone to belittle, they're bully material for the rest of the student body. Worse, if he mentally banishes someone, they become invisible. I am the disappeared.

Pulling myself back to the present, I shudder at the thought that if this had been a weekday, Dad could have been sucked down in one of his trucks, along with his workmates. All while Mayor Brown sat in his office dictating letters and plotting how to spend taxpayers' dollars. Then leaving early for beers with Mr. Toop, who, like past TT execs, Dad believes, makes generous campaign donations to certain organizations in return for their not examining TT policies too closely. In other words, Mica's dad is a TT suck-up, which makes Mica a suck-up's son. On the other hand, TT's really important to our town's economic health, our existence, and with both my parents employed there, I appreciate it as much as anyone.

"Like Dad has any control over Tass geology," Mica says, whipping his dark sunglasses off, picking up a rock, and hurling it into the sinkhole. It cracks the dump truck's sideview mirror, which makes Mica smile. He's wearing ripped black jeans, a tight black T-shirt, a black leather jacket, and the latest runners. "See ya, Chopstick."

He never used to call me names like that. He used to raise his fists to anyone who did.

I've taken to powerlifting lately to help convert my celery-stalk figure to beefcake. As for what my friends call my troll height, I secretly hang from my chin-up bar for fifteen minutes a day in hopes of stretching my body like taffy to attain an altitude at which I can look girls in the eye instead of the shoulder blade. A guy can dream, eh? But my ex-friend hasn't noticed, doesn't care.

I watch as Mica swaggers toward the group, eyes on Ana Toop.

"Hudson?"

"Yes, Mom."

"Will you ever tell me the full story of what happened between you and Mica? You were such good friends. I'm hoping you'll get past whatever it was, at some point."

She sounds like Jett, who would rather be part of a Mica/Hudson/Jett trio over just my new partner-in-training.

I sigh because I feel a little guilty that I've never told her the details. "It was a landslide, Mom. I was sliding down a steep hillside to check out a sinkhole and that triggered a dirt and rockslide. I didn't know Mica was headed towards the sinkhole too, so he was caught in the landslide."

"Okay, that's more than you've given me before. But you were both okay, right? Thanks for finally telling me."

"The dust choked him, and he got some cuts from the rocks that rolled in on him. He thinks I set if off on purpose because he was exploring a passage that he hadn't told me about yet. He had to backtrack all the way to his original entrance underground. I had bruises from my fall. It was scary and dangerous and could have been worse for either of us. But Mom, we'd been arguing more and more before that—about, well, nothing, it seems. Like he was pushing me away. We were growing apart or something. He was changing, turning into kind of a jerk. And no, I did not activate a slide due to his not having invited me along."

She places a hand on my shoulder. "That was months ago, Hudson. It's time you two talked, made up."

"Not that simple," I say, staring at my toes. "He won't have anything to do with me. I don't know why he's grown it into an all-out feud, but—just forget it, Mom. We'll work it out eventually. But that's the story."

"It's like your dad and Lucas," she mumbles so quietly I can hardly hear her. "They fell out as caving partners so long ago. Such a waste of energy, but he won't talk about it."

"I know. All he says is, 'No big deal. Stuff happens.'"

"All the more reason you and Mica don't repeat history."

"Mom, leave it," I say. I don't add that the months-ago misunderstanding got layered with lies, escalating acts of revenge, and a clique-run banishment, essentially.

"Hey!" I sprint away from Mom, waving my arms, and halt a few feet back from the group on the tongue that sticks out over the sinkhole. The group includes Ana. "Five metres back. Not safe there!" I know lots of safety rules, thanks to Dad, even if

I'm a good enough caver that I ignore the occasional one when I feel like it.

Ana's eyes get big, and she starts to back away. Her tall, square-shouldered dad, wearing his Sunday suit and tie, glares at me for the interruption, and Mica's pimply, paunchy father is looking back and forth from me to the hole like a nervous coyote.

"Get back *now!*" I dare to shout as a chunk of dirt from the outcropping skitters down into the wet abyss. Picturing the whole precipice collapsing with the group, I sprint forward just as some safety-vest guys leap forward to yank the men clear. Reaching Ana first, I pull her back, back, back to safety, until I slip, and we tumble into a deep mud puddle, then roll over each other in confusion. We resemble mud wrestlers, but no one's cheering or laughing. Nor do her fiery eyes do anything to help remedy what's left of this disastrous day as she sits up. Mica appears above us and offers her his hand and jacket. She reaches for his hand without a glance at me.

CHAPTER FOUR

"What the heck, Hudson?" Mayor Brown is asking, face pale, looking over his shoulder to the still-intact thumb of land.

"Lucky no one got hurt during the earlier collapse," I say. "Don't need you guys falling in now."

"*You guys?*" Mayor Brown looks like he's going to blow a gasket, his puffy face is so red.

"We were fine," Mica says, eyes narrowed, as Ana takes two steps back from all of us.

"We—meaning those of us in charge—were viewing the damage on *our* property," Mr. Toop enunciates in a slow, stormy tone. "And you are?"

I hear the disdain in his voice, like I'm seriously beneath his rank.

"Hudson Greer, sir," I say, stepping forward and extending my hand. Mr. Toop just directs a hard stare at me. I shrug and lower my arm. "Nice to meet you, Mr. Toop. My dad is one of TT's drivers. Lucky you didn't lose more than one rig. But this sinkhole here is still seriously unstable."

Mr. Toop looks to the foremen gathered, then at his daughter, shivering just feet away. He turns to scowl at me.

"I'm sure my safety officers can take care of things from here, Gear or whoever you are, and I don't appreciate us being interrupted during our inspection. Ana, let's get you home. Lucas, I'll call later," he addresses Mica's dad. "Men, thanks for marking the area with caution tape. Dispatch the firefighters and disperse these crowds as soon as you can, and don't talk to the media."

"But what about a second line of tape at the five-metre mark?" I suggest, feeling bold. "To stop citizens from getting too close and protect you legally if anyone does?" Okay, I'm pushing it, but I've got Ana's attention. She's looking from me to her dad. Mica, on the other hand, looks like he's starting to enjoy the exchange.

"You!" Mr. Toop growls, jabbing a finger at me, his face gone rigid, "get out of my sight right now if you know what's good for you. Men," he adds like he doesn't know or care what their names are, "thanks for coming. Now get to work."

With that, he stalks off, Ana at his side, keeping pace obediently. She's a daddy's girl, I reflect, someone who listens to her father. It's something I can respect since I'm pretty close to my dad as well. And I totally admire my father, given that he is one of the most knowledgeable cavers in the region.

Mica watches Ana go and spits on the ground more or less in my direction. I ignore that and follow my parents downhill.

Mom breaks the silence. "Do you think that's the largest sinkhole we've had since the Big One?"

"For sure," I say.

"Do you think it's from natural causes?" she asks Dad.

"You and I know it probably isn't. Maybe if I shared my maps with TT inspectors."

"No, Dad!" I erupt. "They're not just your maps, and no one gets to see them! You give those to Mayor Brown, and Mica will steal them immediately and then he'll, he'll—" *get famous before me. Apart from me. And lord it over me.*

Dad doesn't bother responding.

"We're going to find that connection, Dad." I grit my teeth. "You, me, and Jett. *That's* when we can tell people what we've discovered, give 'em our maps, let it become a world-famous commercial cave with guides or whatever. A mega cave system that will put Tass and Vancouver Island on the map. A cave that'll teach everyone the importance of cave science," I add, humouring him. "*That's* when we'll go down in history, like the two guys who discovered Kartchner Caverns in Arizona."

I love caving for the possible glory of a new caving find, and I'm never happier than when I'm muddy head to toe and navigating tight, dark spaces like a hyperactive glow-worm.

Dad's shaking his head and pressing his hands to his temples. "I'm going to do some investigating on my own about the cause, Hudson, and we need to ramp up our explorations and expand our maps ASAP on the chance this sinkhole was due to sloppy practices."

My body tenses.

"Careful, honey," Mom says.

"I won't help unless you promise not to share the maps," I say, pulling myself up and folding my arms over my chest. My blood has gone hot. There's no way we've put in all those dark, dirty, dangerous hours the past few years, only to expose our secrets to the whole town before we're ready to propose a commercial cave operation to Parks Canada.

"That is not a promise I can make." Dad's eyes narrow.

I march upstairs in a huff. In the upstairs hallway on the way to my room, I pause outside our den, which is really an old closet, to glance at the scribblings of the region's cave systems thumbtacked all over the wood-panelled wall. There are more in the small grey safe on the floor.

My eyes rove to the desk, to Dad's pride and joy: a shoe-box-sized wooden replica of the church that sank into the ground that fateful day when the Big One killed his father. He made it years ago to honour his father's death, he told me. It took him months to carve the church from aspen, paint it, and complete it with stained-glass windows and a bell in the bell tower that actually rings when you shake the thing. I touch the top of the steeple reverently and try to imagine how it would feel to lose a father so suddenly, unexpectedly, tragically. And not even have his body to grieve over. I understand that making that church helped Dad cope with his grief at the time, and that it's one of his most treasured possessions. But how weird was it to have this masterpiece dominate a room knowing it represents your beloved father's untouched, deeply buried tomb?

I step back from the miniature church and scan the maps on the wall: the Castle passages on the right, the Dungeon catacombs on the left. Reaching out so that my hands touch both walls at once, I feel my fingertips prickle. *There is a connection*, I think. *And we are going to find it.* Then I move on to my room, close the door, and sink down on my bed. Belatedly, I dig into my homework. I refuse to emerge for supper, despite Mom's pleas. *They're my maps too. He can't share them.*

CHAPTER FIVE

I arrive at late-afternoon science class with a bulky backpack sticking out at all angles. I wet my lips with cautious optimism. I had a brainwave last night for today's science project, worked half the night on it, and intend to blow everyone away. Maybe I'll be selected to represent our district at the regional science fair this fall. Maybe I'll win first prize and use the money for slick new caving gear.

"Good morning, class," Mr. Williams starts. "Who would like to go first on their Explain Science project? Remember, you have just three minutes to explain your chosen aspect of science to your classmates in an engaging manner."

"Me," Mica says before I can open my mouth. He stands up, the top buttons of a shiny blue shirt strategically undone, faded blue jeans well fitted.

I slump in my seat.

"And the name of your presentation?" Mr. Williams asks, pen poised over a clipboard.

"Breathing Caves."

I sit up straighter and tuck in the frayed hem of my grey T-shirt.

"In large caves," Mica begins, "pockets of different barometric pressure are forever trying to equalize, and that creates wind. Hold your hands in front of your face, open your mouth as wide as you can, and blow a puff of air onto your palms. Now close your mouth to a small 'O' and do another puff. Which puff did you feel most strongly?"

"The small-mouth puff," Jett says.

"Exactly. Small-mouthed caves have stronger winds than large-mouthed caves, and depending on whether the barometric pressure is rising or falling, that wind can blow out and knock your hat off, or suck it right into the cave." He lifts off his baseball cap and tosses it across the room. It lands at Ana's feet. She looks at it but opts not to pick it up. Here's a new girl pretty enough to have every guy in school crushing on her, but she's too clever, or too smooth, to indicate if she has any interest in return. I admire that. *Take your time, Ana, and above all, don't be fooled by Mica.*

"What's more important," Mica continues, "is that scientists can calculate the volume of a cave by its wind velocity. For instance, at Wind Cave in South Dakota, where the wind has been clocked at more than seventy miles per hour, they know that only ten percent of the cave has been explored. And that, my friends, is just one amazing aspect of science." He checks his watch. "Any questions?"

I raise my hand. His eyes brush over me as he waits for another hand.

"Can they tell from the winds whether Wind Cave and Jewel Cave are connected?" I know the answer. I'm just trying to rattle him.

Mica lifts his chin. "Wind Cave is the world's sixth longest cave and Jewel Cave is the world's third longest cave," he finally declares. "The two are twenty miles apart."

Whereas the Castle and Dungeon are only a stone's throw apart, I muse.

"From wind measurements at both caves," Mica continues, "we know that only ten percent of Wind Cave has been explored, and only three percent of Jewel."

And an estimated thirty percent of Tass's two cave systems have been explored, most of their passages known only to Dad, Mica, and me.

"It takes expert cavers something like four days," Mica continues, "just to get from the entrance to the far end of either Wind or Jewel, and they can't push into new passages faster than about three miles per year. So, it'll be a very, very long time before they know if the two are connected. Plus, even if cracks allow air to flow from one into the other, it doesn't mean a crawling human being can fit through, especially if that crack widens only underwater."

"Smash and blast the stupid crack, and then dive!" suggests Dirk Lamar, one of Mica's suck-ups. One of my apparent replacements as a caving partner.

"Smashing and blasting are strictly against any caver's code unless it's an emergency rescue," I say. "And no one in their right mind would haul cave-diving gear for days through tight passages."

"Except on major international expeditions sponsored by millionaires," Ana inserts. "Like Chevé Cave in Mexico, and Krubera in the Republic of Georgia."

I could faint right here on the spot, knowing just now how deeply Ana is into caving. I've read the same accounts, probably several times each. I'm as passionate about those stories as she obviously is. Only a truly dedicated caver would understand. *Smart, beautiful classmate, look my way. We're meant to be.*

Other heads turn toward Ana as she finishes speaking. But while I can't help but be impressed that she knows about those amazing projects, that kind of expedition sure isn't going to happen in Tass to see if our systems are joined.

"Why would anyone care if caves join up or not?" asks Erin Nakitsas. She's a petite, intense girl with dreadlocks who wears weird outfits, hangs with no one, makes no attempt to blend in, doesn't endorse cliques, and never shirks from strong opinions or sharp questions. She's a straight-A loner, editor of the school paper, and a favourite target of bullies. I've been a jerk to her in the past, like everyone else in the student body, figuring she asks for it. But lately, as a fellow banned person, I've been more intrigued than put off by her quirky personality.

Dirk grins. "Would anyone really care if someone jackhammered through and joined them up?"

Mica's face lights up. "It'd be major money for cave tour operators." Yup, old Mica peeking through—like me, focused on fame. "And we'd maybe discover new species of bats or something," he adds like he's just remembered this is science class.

"Or damage the bat colonies," Ana says. "They're very fussy about airflow, and don't always survive man-made interruptions."

"That's true, Ana," Mr. Williams says. "And if someone artificially breaks through and then one system gets compromised, it can negatively impact water quality in the other." I reflect on Mr. Williams being an environmental activist. I've heard that besides being an awesome science teacher he's particularly focused on water quality. "Hudson, you want to go next?"

I stand and move to the table in the front of the classroom. First, I fill the classroom's electric kettle with water and push the button so it'll boil. Then from my backpack I lift out one prop after another, slowly, with a little flair. From the corner of my eye, I see Ana's eyebrows rise at the sight of a baking sheet, colander, and cardboard egg carton. Mica sneers when I lift out a spray-can of whipping cream, a bag of blueberries, and a jar of maraschino cherries.

Don Gratton, an athletic giant and another of Mica's new caving cohorts, says, "Yum."

"Okay, my presentation is about sinkholes, which involve topsoil sinking into hollows in the ground."

My fellow students' faces go serious.

"The largest sinkhole in the world is the Qattara Depression in Egypt. It's 7,570 square miles, or the size of Lake Ontario, and as deep as a forty-eight-storey building."

Mica drums his fingers on his desk.

"Here on Vancouver Island, the largest sinkhole is Devil's Bath, not far from Tass. It's four-and-a-half city blocks square and thirteen storeys deep. No one knows for sure how deep the Big One here in Tass was, but in 2013, Seffner, Florida suffered a tragedy a lot like it. A bedroom floor actually plunged more than two storeys down: floorboards, furniture, a sleeping man, and all. No one ever recovered his bed or body. The entire room was a deep hole, even as the rest of the house remained standing."

Jett raises an eyebrow. Ana cocks her head. Erin squeezes shut her purple-coloured eyelids and tugs on a beaded braid.

"In some countries where sinkholes are common, farmers place long sticks across their shoulders so that if a crater opens up under their feet, the stick will leave the farmer dangling over it."

A giggle or two.

Anna is sitting up straight and alert, drinking in every one of my words. She smiles as if to encourage me, as if she wants to know more.

"So, let's examine what exactly causes sinkholes. The earth's surface we see here in Tass only looks stable. Really, what's underneath is karst, or limestone, which water dissolves easily over time. That means what's underneath us resembles Swiss cheese.

"It kind of looks like an egg carton," I continue. "See how I place this empty egg carton on a baking sheet. Now I'm opening it so that its lid is on the right, egg holders on the left, the hinge between. I'm now pouring boiling water from Mr. Williams's kettle into the lid. Next, I close the egg carton—flipping the soggy top back over the egg holders, but as I walk my fingers along that solid-looking top surface, my fingers sink through and create one hole after another in the lid. It doesn't take much to punch through when it's wet and there's a hollow just beneath."

"Who cares?" someone says.

"I'll demonstrate with another example." I place the colander on the baking sheet and squirt some whipped cream into the bottom. After dumping a handful of blueberries on top of the cream, I spurt more whipped cream over the blueberries, and finally, set some cherries on the very top.

"The cherries just sit there," I say. "They're not sinking down in. Not yet. Note that in this demo, the whipped cream represents soil, the blueberries are rocks, and the cherries are"—I pause for dramatic effect—"us. In a moment I'll pour boiling water over the concoction and, voilà, we'll be left with just rocks and people all tumbled together at the bottom, with the soil that was holding things up funnelled away deeper into the earth. In fact, the dirt sifts down to other, deeper cavities created by underground waterways or by thousands of years of water seepage."

"Good stuff," Mr. Williams says.

"That water in a karst landscape sets up an area for sinkholes, which can be disastrous and unpredictable. Like yesterday's."

I lift the kettle just as a small flying object comes from centre-left field, hits the kettle, and causes me to lose my grip on it. Boiling water explodes all over my right hand and sears my gut right through my T-shirt. "Aargh!"

The kettle sends the colander and its contents flying to the floor and drenches papers on the teacher's oak desk. I'm holding one reddened hand limply with the other as pain sets my nerves on fire. I look around for what hit me. An eraser.

"Oh my God!" mocks Mica. "Help him, someone! First-aid kit's by the door, Don! Paper towels on the windowsill behind the desk!"

"Hudson, you okay?" Mr. Williams calls out. "Class, settle down. Mica, return to your seat, please."

I charge to the sink and run cold tap water. From the corner of my eye, I glimpse Erin's concerned-looking face and Mica's evil grin. Most of the students look amused as the bell rings and they gather up their books and backpacks. To the sound of shoes shuffling off, I rinse the colander for an excuse to immerse my burned hand in cold water.

"Hudson," Mr. Williams says from behind me as the room goes quiet. "It was a good talk, creative and instructive, with a bit of humour too."

I stare at the floor.

"You have the science right, and the charismatic presence, but I think the presentation was geared for a younger audience, not high schoolers. Certainly not for adults."

"Adults?" My head jerks around. "It wasn't made for adults."

"Exactly. And I think with a little more research and thought, you could do a more sophisticated talk at the townhall meeting Mayor Brown has agreed to this weekend. The one about sinkholes."

"Um, I don't think so," I say. "I mean thanks, but no thanks, even if this one had worked out." I'm picturing myself trying to explain sinkholes to people like Mica's dad, TT employees, and people who've lived here all their lives. People who know way more than I ever will about sinkholes. People who lost relatives in the Big One.

"It'll help persuade me to select you for the regional fall science-fair entry," my teacher says, clicking a ballpoint pen.

I open my mouth to say no, but I'm saved by the next bell.

CHAPTER SIX

Blame it on our cat, Garfield. He was forever staring at the aquarium of goldfish on the kitchen counter, eyes large and tail twitching. At age five, I spent lots of time gawking at the tank too. I mean, hardly anyone else in Tass had an aquarium back then. No big surprise, given you could buy the fish and stuff only in the nearest city, three hours away.

So, one day I pushed a chair against the counter, climbed up, collected the goldfish one by one in a little net, and fed them to Garfield. Hey, I was five.

That's why we have a dusty old aquarium tank stored deep in the junk layers of our garage. It took a while for Mom to find it the day after my science class debacle, after which I carried it delicately, like it was a porcelain bowl full of eggs, to school.

Mr. Williams was hyped. Maybe more excited than me. So was Dad, who offered advice after viewing my pencilled plans in a notebook for the science talk Mr. Williams has arranged for me to do at the community centre meeting about sinkholes.

All this week, I'm working on the presentation in the science lab between classes. I agreed to do it because of the science-fair promise, of course.

Ana steers clear of me, probably because she has heard some of Mica's bull about me: "He's a loser." Or "No one hangs out with him." Testing his credentials as a power-monger and manipulator and trying to clinch her interest for himself. Which pisses me off.

Indeed, my only recent sightings of Ana have been when she's with her father, walking arm-in-arm around TT headquarters. I wonder if that's because they're close or because he's controlling.

"It's called a sandbox model," I explain to Jett as I pour handfuls of dirt, sand, and rocks into the glass tank. It being lunch hour, we're the only occupants of the school lab. "It shows the geology of this region."

"Has Mr. Williams ever tried caving?" Jett asks.

"I asked him, and he said no, he leaves that to the nutcases."

Jett and I smile and add the three ingredients alternately, creating distinct layers, like we're building a parfait at Dairy Queen. Just for the record, Tass is too small for a Dairy Queen. Or anything else other than a gas-station grocery-store/pizzeria and a bar that serves fish and chips.

Every few minutes Jett hands me pieces of egg carton, each a one-egg holder to form a cave.

It's fun poking the cardboard cups into place between the sand and rock layers and seeing them at eye-level, like a cross-section.

"Let's put a little man inside one of the caves, to represent a caver busy exploring," Jett suggests. He grins when I pull out an old plastic soldier from kids' toys my mom keeps around for small visitors.

"Good idea." I chuckle.

When we finish filling the aquarium, we stand back to admire it.

"Now what?" Jett asks, as I'm thinking my whipped-cream, blueberries, and maraschino cherries demo was at least tastier.

"Now we install the town."

"Huh?"

From my beaten-up daypack I pull out small plastic trees from a childhood train set, plus tiny toy cars and a miniature bulldozer from the thrift store, along with thumb-size figures of people, and houses and hotels from a Monopoly set.

Together, Jett and I push the items gently into the top layer of dirt to create a little town. Not exactly a professional architectural model, but it more or less resembles a community.

"Guess what's next?" I ask my friend.

"No idea."

"Well, if we pour enough water over all this, we get a sinkhole." I'm standing there with a full pitcher of water—water is always the culprit when sinkholes form.

"Go for it!" I say, handing Jett the pitcher.

"But we'll ruin everything we just did!"

"We will. And then we'll build it all again to educate the town, impress Mr. Williams, and score my science-fair entry."

Jett tips the pitcher, and water splashes onto the tank's ground cover. Soon it seeps through the dirt and charges through the sand. Droplets explore the caves, saturate their carton contours, and dribble downward. I watch, mesmerized, as the undergirding of Tass sags like a sandcastle in an incoming tide. I can't help grinning when a hole forms in the middle of the aquarium's contents.

"A new mega-cave! And that's exactly how some caves are formed, over millions of years, even," I enthuse.

The houses and trees begin to tip toward the centre, above the newly formed middle-earth gap.

"All right!" we cheer, caught up in the moment.

Another half-pitcher of water and—*bam!* The whole town folds in on itself, collapses, and dives deep, like water headed down a drain, like sand pouring through an hourglass. Monopoly houses and hotels, upended toy people, toppling trees all feed into the giant new crater. At the same time, the disintegrating rim of the hole rains sand into the open-air grotto, forming a doughnut shape of dirt and granules as it buries people like avalanche victims. Bodies fortunate enough to have fallen into the centre of the cave floor remain visible.

In other words, the parfait is a ghastly mess. What we spent half an hour creating has just been destroyed.

"So that, ladies and gentlemen, is a sinkhole," I announce to an imaginary audience, taking a bow.

But as I stare at the aquarium's chaos, a bolt of pain strikes my chest. The plastic figures could be my own friends and family. My mind flashes to the church model on my father's desk. The church sank out of sight with no warning, like an elevator with cut cables, taking an entire congregation with it. My father has been grieving ever since.

It plunged too far down even to find. The bodies were never recovered. I can almost hear the hymn-singing turning into ghastly screeches. Now, on moonlit nights, wisps of ghosts are said to float through the memorial garden at the site, singing sorrowfully amongst the shrubs and flowers. Doomed to a too-early, too-deep grave. A chill runs down my spine as Mr. Williams enters the room.

"Looking good, Hudson."

"Last week's sinkhole was not natural, right?" I ask him.

"Exactly," he replies. "The Big One could happen again."

But I'm only doing this to get my science-fair entry form, I remind myself.

"What we're not showing," Mr. Williams says, a frown creeping onto his face, "is the aquifer."

"The aquifer?" Jett asks.

"An underground stream that people drill their wells into.

It's where we get our drinking water. Technically, an aquifer is a body of porous rock way underground that lets water flow. Maybe set your entire aquarium on a shallow glass baking dish of water with blue food-colouring in it."

I stare at our aquarium mess. I'd better get major points for putting in all this time and effort. At least my parents have promised a pizza night out to celebrate my talk.

"Why blue food-colouring?" Jett asks.

"To show our aquifer is pure," he says. "In fact, it's magically clear in these parts, world class. The porous rocks purify it. Unless—"

"Unless?"

"Unless there are pollutants and debris in the water from a landslide or badly built road. Then disastrous sinkholes can happen."

"Don't tell me we have to cut a hole in the bottom of the aquarium to make the blue water go cloudy," I say as Jett rolls his eyes.

Mr. Williams pats me on the shoulder. "No, Hudson, I think you can just explain that a compromised aquifer can be a side effect of bad logging practices."

"Hmm, this is a science demo, not a political rant, remember?" TT is my parents' employer, a respectable company that everyone in town appreciates. In fact, this simple science demo could imply TT is bad. Could make enemies for me of Mayor Brown and TT people. Or push Ana and Mica farther away.

Mr. Williams flashes a too-quick smile. "You're right, just stick to the science. You're going to be a sensation."

I relax. Yup. Me, science, and caving. The perfect formula for eventual fame as a cave guide, and to impress Ana. Let's just say it's not the pizza I'm doing this for.

CHAPTER SEVEN

My demo, "The Science of Sinkholes," goes almost exactly as planned. The mostly adult audience—no Mica, thankfully, but Ana is there—smiles at the little houses, trees, and cars, and listens as I explain the geology and point out the cardboard egg-cup caves positioned randomly within the layers. Erin sits way at the back in some weird outfit that looks like a sari over pyjama bottoms. Her braids are pulled into a bun, and she scribbles busily in a notebook whenever I pause. What's her thing? Coming up with good stories? She intrigues me.

"Now, let's add a little more water than the region is used to." I love how all eyes are locked on me. Adults in town don't heed the Mica-run high-school banishment code, so I'm alive and visible here. I'm wearing my best jeans and hoodie, and two insoles in each of my shoes for some fake height. "Perhaps there's a flood, or a deluge after a drought."

"Or," Mr. Williams adds from his seat, "disturbance to the system from a new road built too close to a stream." That prompts frowns on a few audience members' faces. "Or from over-removal of trees, since their roots are key to holding back water." Now a few people have turned in their seats to locate the person so rudely interrupting me.

I cough to pull attention back to the front of the room and slowly pour the water into our masterpiece. Again, it trickles down, fills little cavities, and keeps moving as the sand and soil begin to shift.

The model town tilts and sinks, and some little kids in the audience cheer and clap. Adults seem divided into those smiling politely, and those shifting in their seats. How many are remembering their relatives trapped in the plummeting church?

I spot Erin with her hand up and point to her with a smile.

"What would we as citizens do if we got swallowed by a sinkhole?" she asks. "Is there any chance of survival?"

"Glad you asked," I say, ignoring Mayor Brown's frown. "Depends how deep it is, of course. In a cover-collapse sinkhole, which is the fastest and most dangerous kind, you may have only seconds to leap clear when the cracks start forming in front of you. If you can't jump away, you need to cover your head, tuck your knees together, fall on your side, and roll backward. It's called the parachute landing fall and evenly distributes the shock of an impact. You really don't want to land flat on your back or head."

"Then what?" she asks.

"Stay low and small and try to find a safe spot. Don't try to climb out, because the edges are unstable, and your activity could cause debris to fall from above. Keep injured people calm. If you have a cellphone, call for help. First responders know how to rig rope rescues from high angles and lower rescue harnesses and slings—"

"Nicely done, Hudson," Mayor Brown says, standing abruptly. He's wearing red suspenders to hold his trousers up beneath his big stomach. "I can see you're going to be a great scientist—or Emergency Services crew member!" He laughs like the latter is a joke. "Who helped you with this little project, anyway?"

"Jett and Mr. Williams," I say, beaming. "And Dad, a little." My chest thuds a belated warning. Should I have said I'd done it all by myself? Could I get Dad and my teacher in trouble, especially after Mr. Williams's comments?

I sit down quickly, because apart from my little show, the townhall meeting is all about the recent sinkhole, and what could or should be done about sinkhole dangers in these parts.

Dad sits alert but unusually still in his seat, Mom folds and unfolds her hands beside him. Mr. Williams answers some questions about the science of sinkholes. So does Mr. Toop, who, it turns out, is a trained geologist. Ana looks bored as she fiddles with her cellphone despite evil eye looks from her dad. Erin keeps taking notes.

I remind myself I've just given an awesome presentation to the whole town and try to come down from my high by staring at the ceiling. That means I find myself studying several cracks where the walls and ceiling join.

I flash back to a conversation with Mr. Williams while we were discussing my presentation after school one day.

"By gathering all this information, do you realize you're proving that the parking-lot sinkhole was probably caused by TT's lousy logging practices?"

"We don't know that!" I retort, jaw clenched.

"Don't we?" he asks. *"Have you walked around the community centre lately?"*

"Huh?"

"New cracks in the foundations are spreading, and there's a small, shallow-bowl depression in the backyard mostly hidden by tall weeds. Those are two warning signs of a future sinkhole. Plus, the well on the property has dropped to drought levels—a possible sign of leakage into an underground water cavity."

A part of me—a part of the whole town—knows that the parking-lot sinkhole may have been caused by TT activity. And the company might be doing stuff that will cause more damage. But suspecting and proving a connection are two very different things. *And both my mom and dad work for TT.*

Bathroom break needed. I slip down the aisle and find the steps to the basement restrooms. Unable to find the lights, I keep walking through the dim, mouldy-smelling space to the sound of creaking and groaning around me. It's only the pipes, I tell myself. But that's yet another sign of a coming sinkhole, I read somewhere.

When I go to wash my hands, the old faucet spurts out cloudy water, and not much of it. Not good. Mr. Williams said the property's well level is dropping.

After the bathroom visit, I feel a need for fresh air. Finding a rear door unlocked, I step outside to the overgrown backyard of the centre. There, I push my way through wilting, waist-high weeds—odd given recent rains. Vegetation begins to die when a hidden sinkhole drains away water, I remember. A tree with an old tire-swing on it has drooped so much that the tire touches the ground. I stumble when the ground plunges unexpectedly downhill. It's just a little bowl-shaped depression, no big deal. Instinctively, I circle it looking for a hole that might lead to a cave. Imagine making a new discovery right here in town! For sure it's the dip my science teacher claimed might be a sinkhole tipoff.

Oops. I realize the presentation is about to wrap up, and people might be wondering where I am. As I slink up the steps and take my seat again, Mayor Brown is at the podium.

"Well, thank you, everyone, for coming, and you'll be pleased to know that Mr. Toop and I have arranged to bring in an inspector who will examine the causes of Sunday's unfortunate little sinkhole and advise us to ensure we are adhering to the industry's most rigorous safety practices. That, in turn, will make sure our town's water supply remains pure for many years to come."

Good. That should satisfy Mr. Williams. Let the inspector deal with all this. I try to catch Ana's eye, but she's staring at her phone, looking seriously uninterested in anything going on around her and perhaps annoyed at being dragged here by Daddy. As good-looking as she is, I have to wonder about her for a second. Like, why is she bored? This is important stuff, to everyone in town, especially her dad's company.

Reflecting on how well my demo went, I smile tentatively at Mr. Williams, who grins back. Science talk done and well received. Meeting a success. Now Dad, Jett, and I can get back to caving. Underground, where my life usually goes better than up here.

CHAPTER EIGHT

Jett and I are sipping Slurpees in front of the gas station the next day when I catch movement on a hill behind the park: a familiar figure wearing rubber boots and a coverall, carrying a caving helmet, and sporting a waterproof waist-pack. He's heading west of town.

"That's Mica," I say. "With full caving gear, from the looks of it."

"Alone?" Jett squints in that direction.

"Probably meeting others," I guess. "Want to follow him?"

"You mean shadow him like spies? Come on, you two. Enough already. We should all be caving together." One look at my face and Jett winces like he knows he just overstepped.

"We are going to follow him to see if he's onto a cave entrance we don't know about yet," I say through gritted teeth.

Jett's shoulders slump and he looks away from me. We chug our Slurpees, toss the recyclable cups, and start a stealth march. We keep Mica within sight while ensuring we're out of his vision the odd time he turns around. A fifteen-minute slog later, he halts beside a cliff fronted by ferns, moss, and nettles. He crouches down with his back to the rock wall and scans the horizon in all directions, including our way, though we're well hidden. Like he's looking for someone.

"What do you bet he's waiting for Dirk and Don," I say in a hushed voice. "At least I hope he's not caving by himself." Not sure why I even care.

Jett shoves some gum in his mouth as we wait for something to happen. The object of our attention, apparently unaware of us, looks antsy—he squirms, tosses rocks, and frowns. Fifteen minutes into our wait, he stands, scans the hillside again, and kicks a stone down the slope. Then he turns and disappears. Yup. Dives into the ground, like the ferns have just swallowed him whole.

I grab Jett by his sweatshirt sleeve. "Must be an entrance there. Can't believe he's going into a cave *by himself.* That's nuts."

"His funeral," Jett says, plucking a blade of grass from beside him.

"We should follow him."

"You just want to see where that opening goes, dude. And it's not gonna happen, 'cause we don't have gear."

Busted. Jett is right, of course. He stretches out full length on the ground like sunbathing is now in order.

"Jett!"

"What, man?"

"I'll be back really fast with two helmets. Stay here, and don't let anyone see you if he comes out, or if the other guys show up."

Jett sighs, seems about to object, then says, "Hey, there are three of us. Mica, you, and me." He looks triumphant for a second, then adds slyly, "Even if Mica doesn't know we're on his tail. Okay, get the gear already." And he shuts his eyes, a new blade of grass tucked between his lips like he's trying out for the hillbilly role in a movie.

"No one has come, no one has gone," he reports twenty minutes later when I sprint up, forehead dripping sweat, helmets in hand.

"Okay, we're going in, then."

"To protect Mica, not to plant a flag in his new find," comes the stern reply.

I nod gravely and Jett accepts the helmet I hand him and follows me to the ferns. The opening is so small I don't know how Mica ever found it, but my body fits if I stretch my hands ahead of me and wriggle in like a worm. I hear grunts and curses behind me as Jett plays second, larger worm.

The rocky passage opens up as we travel along, eventually depositing us into a chamber the size of a dome tent that stops at the edge of a pond the size of a campfire. It's a musty, damp space with no way out but the way we came in. Rounded stone walls above and to the sides of the pond declare a dead end.

"Mica must have come out while you were sleeping, Jett."

"I was not sleeping, and he did not," Jett says, eyebrows knitted, voice full of concern.

"He wouldn't dive into a sump with no safety backup." A sump is a tunnel fully filled with water. As in, super dangerous because no caver can know how big it is, how long it is, how sharp the rocks are in it, and if there's any breathing space the other side.

"Wouldn't he?" Jett asks, meeting my eyes.

It's been a while since I caved with Mica. The old Mica wouldn't have. But the new one, from what I've seen, has grown into an ambitious egomaniac more likely to take stupid risks. It's all about Dad-became-mayor back in December and had no more time for son, who can't live up to Dad-on-a-pedestal but has learned how to use it for whatever new purposes he dreams up. Sad and shallow, in my private opinion, but a small part of me feels sorry for him too. Meanwhile, his mom has gotten so busy attending events with her husband that she has spent way less time keeping an eye on Mica. He told me that with bitterness even before we got into our feud. Power corrupts, they say. Evident in all three Brown family members, it seems to me.

But where is Mica? A sixth sense tells me something has gone wrong. It has been the better part of an hour since he disappeared. What if he's in trouble? There are a million ways a siphon, or sump, can mess up a caver or take his life, even with a support team. Mica may not be my caving partner anymore, not even my friend at the moment, but he doesn't deserve—

Spotting a pile of clothes to one side—Mica's—I strip to my boxers and step into the pool.

"Don't you dare, Huds."

I dive before Jett can say another word; before he can talk sense into me.

It's cold but not freezing as I submerge, and murky in the silty water, even with my headlamp. It's also claustrophobically tight and nasty-sharp in the tunnel, like it's lined with metal studs designed to scrape my skin raw. My helmet bumps into rocks that stick down from the ceiling like icicles, reminding me why cavers wear helmets. There's not enough room to turn around, but I'm saving enough breath to back out if I have to. Like maybe Mica didn't.

I pull myself along the rocky bottom like a salamander, willing there to be an end to this watery passage, an opening with a ceiling high enough to provide oxygen, maybe a ledge to stop and sit on and catch my breath. A ledge where Mica will be sitting, greeting me with, *Hey, Huds! You found it too. I think it continues on to great places. Want to carry on exploring with me? Let's leave that incident behind us, what do you say? It was all a silly misunderstanding. I apologize.*

My lungs are complaining, telling me in urgent terms to back up, when I see two small, vertical logs ahead. Their bottoms are lodged between small boulders in the hazy water. One jerks. It resembles what the Mafia might call a leg in a concrete boot. Frantically scanning upward, I identify a body, naked except for boxers, a body that ends at the neck.

I break the surface, my helmet bumping the ceiling, and gasp in an air pocket that's no wider than an arm's length to the front, back, and sides of me, my lips just above water. I screech as a head with bugged-out eyes bobs in front of me.

"Huds!" Mica screams, even though his face is mere inches from mine. "Help me! Rock fell on my left foot! I'm trapped! Can't move! Running out of breath!" He's saying all this through seriously chattering teeth, his voice amplified in our microspace.

I lift an arm to rest it on his shoulder, since calming a victim is the most important first step in rescuing him. And maybe because I need to calm myself from the fright of finding him like this. Just beyond our heads, the passage plunges back below water level. It's like we're in a bubble-shaped skylight with water up to our chins.

"You're not running out of air," I say in as steady a voice as I can manage. "And you're not stuck, just temporarily—"

"Screw you! I'm stuck and I'm going to drown!" he shouts, throwing my arm off him like I'm making things worse.

"Mica," I say with forced calm. "Breathe slowly, count to ten, and I'll have you free. Got it?"

He nods his head, which causes him to swallow a bit of water. His eyes are squeezed shut, but he doesn't resist.

I curl up like a snail, dive down, and place my hands around the rock. There's no room to manoeuvre, would be no room for anyone but me and my shrimpy frame to get where hands are needed. But I'm determined. Mothers pull cars off their infants in a crisis, right? Superhuman strength comes when you need it.

I pull, yank, and kick to keep myself on the bottom, and attack the rock again. Up for air, down again, attack double-strength, up for air, down again, attack like a Marine Corps officer. Finally, it loosens enough that Mica's foot comes free, at which point his fleshy knee comes up and accidentally hits me on the chin. Bubbles trail out of my mouth. I turn into a curled-up slug, and the disturbance to the gravel on the bottom totally messes with my sight. It's full-out panic when I realize I'm out of breath with no sense of where up or down are.

Then strong hands clamp on either side of my helmet and yank me up like someone's tackling me in a football game. I gasp in our oxygen pocket.

"What are you doing here?" comes a recovered voice. "You actually followed me in, you jerk?"

"You're welcome," I say, my voice flat and muted. "Are you okay?"

He stares at me, shoulders quaking, lips pressed together like new and old Mica are fighting to decide on a response.

"Thanks." And he disappears underwater just like that, pushing me against the sharp wall on his way back to the entry tunnel, kicking up froth as he heads back toward the pond's shore.

I sigh, if only as preparation for loading myself up with more oxygen, and stare curiously in the other direction, wondering whether the next sump is swimmable, whether there's another air pocket on its far side, whether the route continues to where the Castle and Dungeon meet in a top-secret chamber filled with exotic formations the shape of high priests or priestesses blessing the confluence of waters.

But my teeth are chattering, and my body is shuddering, so I lower my face back into the sump and follow Mica's bubbly trail. What I don't expect, when I flop onto the pond's flat rocky "beach," is a huddle of guys blocking the dry passageway beyond, roughing up Jett and shouting with an anger that echoes off black walls.

"Stop it!" I say, scrambling up and throwing myself into the melee. "Leave Jett alone!"

"You too?" Dirk growls. "Following Mica, trying to leapfrog ahead to steal our find again? What'd you do, mangle his ankle to slow him down? Try to drown him?"

I look to Mica, whose back is turned to me as he pulls his clothes onto his shaking frame, and I note blood seeping from his ankle through his trousers. He wavers ever so slightly, and Dirk catches him by the elbow and leads him toward the exit.

"If he's hypothermic, you need to get him home ASAP," I say as the others stare at me.

"We'll do that, no thanks to you, asswipe," Don says. "Can't find your own passages, so you have to barge into ours? Follow us again and you'll find there's not enough space in these caverns for both of us to exit in one piece."

The three are gone before I can shake my head. My heart feels heavy, like it's weighed down by a rock. I can't banish an image, a fantasy, of this all having gone differently: thankfulness, apologies, hugs, reconciliation.

"What happened? Are you okay?" Jett hands me my clothes as he tilts his head back to slow a fist-induced nosebleed. "And does the passage lead anywhere?"

"Leads to trouble," I say. "Are you okay?"

"Yup."

I did what I had to do. It wasn't about leapfrogging. But what Mica and his gang believe is as unyielding as these cavern walls. Maybe we'll never find the crack required to reach one another.

"Let's get out of here. I'll explain later."

CHAPTER NINE

"Pizza tonight," Mom reminds me with a broad smile when I get home from school.

"Yay." I dump the contents of my school locker on the kitchen table. Lots of school stuff, because today was the last day of school. Hello, summer!

Tonight's pizza outing is my parents' reward for shining (ha!) at the community centre meeting. Well, the presentation didn't blow up, and maybe it even shone some light into curious minds, so there you go.

Being the start of summer break, almost everyone I know is going to a party at Mica's tonight, but Don cornered me point-blank after a morning class to declare, "You're not invited, just so you know. Don't go trying to crash it, Twig. Go hang with your dork friend instead."

He meant Jett, which confirms my suspicion that Jett wasn't invited either. Jett's social life, if he ever had one, has suffered from being my sidekick, even though I think he figured Mica and I would have ended our standoff long ago and let him join us as a third hand. Then again, he kind of accepts what is; he's one of those guys who floats through high school without seeming to see cliques, attract trouble, or care who he's hanging with. Enviable in that way. Anyway, I'm increasingly glad I tapped him for replacement caving companion. He has fast-growing caving skills and good instincts, as well as a sense of humour and an even temper.

So, parental-time-with-pizza is where I'm at tonight. At least my parents are okay. Wouldn't want Mica's loud, pushy dad and socialite mom, for instance. Or Ana's stern powerhouse of a father. But rumour has it *she's* going to the party. Which means maybe I'll sneak in later after all. Mica will be annoyed but not surprised and not likely to actually kick me out. I hope.

Mom's voice pulls me back to the present. "Dad says it's light enough out these evenings to fit in a short hike before we hit Tass Gas Pizza. Stretch our legs, work up an appetite, see how much water is spilling over Ribbon Falls. Okay with you?"

Tass Gas Pizza is a pretty hilarious name for a side window at the gas station teamed with a picnic table that doesn't take reservations. As for Ribbon Falls, well, it's one of the few cascades in the region without a cave carved out behind it, so it's never my first pick. But then again, this isn't about caving and there's time before Mica's party starts.

"Sounds good, Mom. When's Dad home?"

"Here!" comes a booming voice from the doorway as he removes his hardhat and leans down to unlace his workboots. "Pizza for our budding scientist, I hear. And a meander up the mountain beforehand." He claps me on the back because he gets that I'm too old for a hug. I head for my room to change my clothes.

Tromping up the forest trail a short while later, I smell the sweet scent of summer in the air and glimpse swallows dipping in and out of view. We come to an old arched footbridge over the creek, one Mom likes so much she has photographed it lots of times.

"This was made by a pioneer stonemason," Mom tells us, as if she hasn't said so a bunch of times before.

I roll my eyes, and she smiles.

"The trapezoid-shaped stone in the middle is called a keystone. It allows all the rocks to fit together and hold forever without cement or bolts," she muses.

"Feel good to be done with school?" Dad asks as we carry on upstream.

"Of course. More caving time."

A startled deer leaps away as we round a corner. Soon, the roar of nearby Ribbon Falls fills our ears.

"How's work?" I ask. "When's that TT inspector coming 'round?" I've been thinking about TT practices more since the community centre meeting.

Dad frowns. "Was supposed to come this week, but got delayed, they said. Today we got the go-ahead to back those machines out of the new parking lot so we don't lose any more if the sinkhole crumbles at the edges. That starts tomorrow. About time, I say, but I'm just a joe, you know."

"One of the smarter, more senior joes," Mom assures him. "It's top secret, but I can tell you we're hiring ten new workers next month. And I cut a cheque today for travel expenses regarding an inspector travelling here next week, so that just proves TT really does care about safety and its employees."

"Love having an in-house spy in the admin office. What's his name?" Dad asks, pecking Mom on the cheek, then turning his head as the thundering falls come into view. "Wow, look at what recent rains have done to our little Ribbon."

"It's confidential," Mom teases. "So, I can't tell you what *her* name is."

"A female inspector?" Dad looks genuinely surprised. "I know most of the Island's inspectors and have never come across a woman. Not that I care—only about her credentials and objectivity."

"Exactly, dear." Mom pulls his faded, floppy hiking hat off his balding head and tosses it like a Frisbee toward the falls' pool.

"Got it!"

We all turn in surprise to see a soaking-wet hiker with the hat in his hands, water streaming down his fully clothed body.

"Mr. Williams?" I say. "Did you just step through the falls?"

"Either that or I'm in the habit of hiking up here right after I take a shower in my clothes." He winks and tosses the hat back to Dad. Then his eyes dart around, as if to confirm it's just my parents and me. Or maybe he's not so pleased to have run into us and caught the hat.

"How's it going, Mal?" Dad asks.

"It's going, Colm. Enjoying the longer evenings?"

"We are," Mom says, but her eyes are on a huge backpack we hadn't previously noticed to the side of the falls.

"Is that a training pack?" I ask. Sometimes serious hikers fill their packs with sand and water jugs and put in lots of distance to train for serious expeditions. Why else would anyone have a massive pack just ten minutes up-mountain from town?

Mr. Williams's face goes an interesting shade of pink. "Um, yeah, just trying to whip the old body in shape, Hudson."

He rests his hands on a jumbo-sized water bottle in a belt holder around his waist and wipes a free hand across his wet forehead. Then he steps out of the water and moves toward his pack. Or more like in front of it, as if to block our view, which makes me tilt my head to get a better look at it. One bulge in the ripstop nylon suggests there's a box inside. Other, more rounded lumps indicate cylindrical-shaped things.

"How much does it weigh?" I ask casually, stepping around him and stooping to lift the pack.

He whirls around to stop me, but not before what looks like a black toolbox tumbles out. It's not shut tightly, so the lid springs open and spills out a collection of small bottles, glass slides, medicine droppers, and stoppered test tubes. Deeper in the pack I spot a device that looks like a giant calculator a person could barely get a hand around.

I look up. "A chemistry set?"

"Smart kid," he says with less than full enthusiasm. "A field kit that tests water chemistry for pH, chlorine, copper, phenols, detergent surfactants, and turbidity. Can never be too concerned about how clean our drinking water is, eh?"

That contradicts the training-pack reply. Not that I'm about to point it out.

"I think we're lucky in this region," Dad says. "Water reports are consistently good around here. All that limestone filters our groundwater before it hits the aquifer."

"Exactly! We are fortunate, aren't we? It's just a little hobby of mine, making sure it's all good," my teacher says.

"Well, enjoy the evening, Mal," Mom says. "We're just stretching our legs before dinner."

"Sorry for spilling your stuff," I add. "Want me to help you put it all back in?" There's a black foam lining in the box with special indentations for each bottle. At least nothing broke rolling onto the grass.

"I'm fine, thanks. You enjoy your walk too," he says cheerfully. "See you next week for more science-fair prep."

We've been meeting up regularly, and I'm pretty excited to be representing my district in the fall science fair. "I can't wait for the fall—"

"Actually," he says, "I should mention, I'm not teaching in the fall."

The three of us pause and study him. He's fiddling with his pack's drawstring and doesn't look up. He hesitates, then says, "They're looking into a replacement science teacher."

Given that Mr. Williams is one of those rare, good teachers, losing him would be bad. "For how long?" I ask.

He glances up and looks from my mom to my dad. "Maybe for good, maybe just a few months. Depends. I have a meeting with the school board next week."

Mom and Dad exchange glances. "For getting on TT's case at the sinkhole meeting?" Dad asks, going suddenly still.

"Of course not," comes the reply, served up with a smile. "It's my decision."

Dad tries to question Mr. Williams further, but my teacher just shakes his head. "Can't say anything else at this stage, sorry." The awkward silence is broken by the *rat-a-tat-tat* of a piliated woodpecker.

"Okay, see you," we finally say, as Mom ushers us down the trail. Twigs snap underfoot, shadows fall, and the quiet of the forest envelops us. I go quiet while contemplating all kinds of questions and vague notions. Luckily, my growling stomach helps distract me.

When we finally get to the pizza that evening, it doesn't taste as good as usual. We each pull a piece out of the box and start nibbling slowly.

"He says it's his choice, but I wonder," Dad begins.

Mom raises the pizza to her mouth. "It will be a great loss for the school, but let's talk about something else."

"Um, Mom, Dad, I forgot to mention I'm going to a party tonight, at Mica's house."

"How nice! Celebrating the end of the school year, of course! I knew you two would make things right one of these days. I presume his parents will be home?" Mom asks.

"For sure." Actually, I have no idea about that.

"Okay, call if you want a ride home, no questions asked."

Hmm. No questions—unless the call is ten minutes after I arrive there, or I'm waiting for them on the curb with a broken nose.

CHAPTER TEN

The ground vibrates with pounding music, and every light in the big white house is on as I approach.

A rush of memories greets me: years of hanging out here. Hide-and-seek, after-school snacks (under the watchful eye of Mica's nanny), backyard pup-tent overnights (spooked by his big brother), and homework sessions (where Mica mostly managed to get me to do his for him). Also, gearing up for cave explorations (where I got to borrow Mica's better equipment), and popping popcorn or playing Monopoly with his parents, brother, and him, like I was part of their family. Back when their family did family time together. Before his dad became mayor.

And later, contests as to who could hold their breath longer in the hot tub, who could displace the most water while diving from the board into the pool, and fervent late-night discussions about music, girls, and more. More recently, of course, female schoolmates in the hot tub with us, and Pepsis replaced by smuggled beer.

Kids are laughing, shouting, and dancing on the rear patio, which butts up against a rockface that Mica and I spent our childhoods learning to boulder on. A high dirt cliff above the stone slab is too steep to scramble up, as we know better than anyone. Tonight, someone has strung sparkly lights across the rockface, and there's a tin tub of ice and beer pushed up against it. A gift from Mica's older brother? Clearly their parents aren't home. The mayor and his wife would definitely not turn a blind eye to underage drinking in their home.

I walk across the patio and help myself to a beer, pop the top, and enjoy a soothing swallow. It dawns on me that everyone who's not in the pool or hot tub is in costume. And here's me in my jeans. Guess I didn't get the message on my party invite, mostly because I lacked a party invite.

"Hey, Hudson!" breathes an unsteady girl whose name I can't remember. Perfect. At least one person here has spoken to me.

"Hey," I reply. Small groups pass me, glance my way, take on a veiled look, and keep moving. It's interesting to be invisible. I tell myself there are worse options. Then I note the worse option: some students pointing at me and whispering.

"Hi, Heather." I approach a girl standing on her own, leaning against the back wall of the house in the shadows, vaping. She seems overdressed in a sparkling evening gown with high heels, but what do I know about fashion?

"Hudson," she says uneasily, and scans the crowd until her eyes rest on Mica, who is hobbling about in a fake tux. "Mica is limping, you know."

"Mmm. A little."

"Did you really hurt him while you guys were caving, because you wanted to get ahead of him?"

"What? Of course not. Is that what everyone's saying?"

She gives me a grim look and walks to one of the pockets of students staring at me with hostility, like she doesn't want demerits for hanging with an accused subterranean assaulter.

Seriously? This is what I have to deal with tonight? And after I risked my life to save Mica?

I look around for anyone far enough distant from Mica's golden gang constellation to risk indulging in conversation with a small planet fallen out of orbit. This banishment thing wouldn't work in a larger school. But there aren't many in our high school, which makes cliques and unspoken edicts ironclad.

A gaggle of bikinied girls leap into the pool with exuberant shouts. I raise my beer to them and get giggles in return. Oh wait, they're giggling at Erin, who glides by in fortune-teller garb, something round clutched under one arm. She actually looks good in a rainbow-coloured, flouncy, layered skirt, off-the-shoulders peasant blouse, and wide buckled belt. A purple scarf tied around her head emphasizes the length and shiny darkness of her braids, and a dozen coin-style necklaces jangle at her bodice.

She doesn't pause to talk to anyone, and no one engages her. She floats gracefully through the clutches of partiers like a contented phantom. Perhaps she's here on reconnaissance, doing a social studies paper on the various methods teenagers employ to ignore someone in their midst deemed unworthy to talk to. I've just doubled her available study subjects on that.

"Hudson." She pauses and smiles, which gives me an unexpected wave of relief. "What are you supposed to be?" She sets down a cheap crystal ball she's carrying around.

"Just me. Didn't know the dress code."

"Because you, like me, were among the uninvited. But you're here now, so let me tell you I enjoyed your science demonstrations last week. Both of them. It took balls, especially the second one in front of TT brass. Didn't know you had any."

"Um… thanks?"

"I'm not buying the line about you trying to drown Mica on the weekend, by the way. Although there were witnesses, I understand." She taps the sparkly globe and gazes blandly up at me. Given that she's only five-foot-and-a-bit, she may be the only classmate in Tass who makes me feel tall.

"Unreliable witnesses are dangerous," I manage to reply. "But I never expected Mica to admit I actually saved his life."

"I see. But that was after breaking the almighty Cave Code that says Thou Shalt Not Steal Someone Else's Lead. Or so I'm told."

"There's also a code that says no one caves alone. Minimum of three for safety."

"Mica plus D-squared wasn't three?" she asks, using Don's and Dirk's hated merger nickname.

"Mica entered long before they arrived. I went in to see if Mica was okay. When D-squared got there, they pummelled Jett, who was waiting for me while I rescued Mica. That's all in case you're quoting anyone for the *Tass High School Gazette*."

"Whatever," she says, shrugging in a way that makes her coin necklace jangle and swirling to show off her flowy skirt. "I'm off duty tonight, and believe it or not, the caving community's shenanigans are not worthy of dispatching an investigative reporter. Anyway, in my personal opinion, you and Mica are pathetic," she adds, sweeping her eyes vaguely in Mica's direction. He's on the other side of the pool doing a headstand for a cheering audience. "You're like moose locking antlers in a life-and-death struggle for dominance."

I chuckle. "Glad the *Gazette* gives you moments off, and you're absolutely right that the fractured caving community doesn't warrant a drop of ink. So, what are the highlights of tonight's party so far, Fortune-teller Erin? I like your costume, by the way. Suits you." Will she take that as a compliment or insult? Erin and her razor-sharp intelligence and wit always make me nervous. In fact, this is one of the longer exchanges we've had in all the years we've jointly attended Tass schools—as in, since second grade. Let's just say we've never travelled in the same circles, even if Tass circles are microscopic.

"Thank you. Events you have so far missed: a contest for dive-bombing into the pool, won by Dirk. A competition for scaling the boulder, victor being Mica. A special demo involving using mature ivy to immaturely climb up to that second-storey balcony, then leaping into the pool without splatting on the pool deck enroute. Don ruled. And the discovery of a bottle of vodka that induced more symptoms of Tass male rivalry and latent imbecility."

I laugh, pleased she's so funny. "That implies the females have been behaving themselves," I say, watching the drunk bikini clan attempt to simulate synchronized swimming. "So, not taking notes or photos?"

"Not I." There's an awkward pause, and I have a flash of fear she's going to saunter off.

"Aren't you going to tell me my fortune?" I point to her ball.

Erin smiles and rubs the globe vigorously.

CHAPTER ELEVEN

"**You will live a long and healthy life**—*if you stop caving*," Erin says.

I laugh again. "Not gonna happen. What else?"

"Actually, I'm more into shrinking heads than revealing the future. Dare me to analyze your personality?"

"Go for it." I grin.

"Your fractious relationship with a certain other caver in Tass is less about the landslide episode than it is about the fact that, without each other, your mutual chances of making noted cave discoveries are diminished. It's also about you being jealous of his money and popularity—"

"What?"

"—and him being jealous of your smarts and your doting, devoted parents. The whole happy-happy *WandaVision* family thing." She's smirking.

"My family? What's that got to do with anything?"

"You asked me to put you on a sofa."

"No, I didn't. And it's not his popularity. It's his power. His power-mongering and manipulation." My face goes hot.

She cocks her head. "People have power over you only if you give them permission to."

Awkward pause.

"Oh, and a philosopher into the bargain too," I say, trying for a jokey tone but hearing an edge of bitterness. As if she knows anything about anything. All she's done is confirm my theory that she's an oddball, an enigma wrapped in a riddle.

"So that's what the bad vibes between you and Mica are all about? A landslide?"

I spin around to realize Ana has appeared behind us and been listening in. Only now do I catch the scent of her subtle, jasmine-smelling perfume.

Her straight face is framed by a stretchy tiger costume, complete with ears and whiskers on its full-face hood. "Hi, Hudson. Hi, Erin," she says.

Erin nods curtly.

"Hello Ana," I say, heart hammering. "Sounds like you've caught up on gossip pretty fast for a new girl." My lungs emit a too-audible sigh. Of course she'd have been briefed by now. "A landslide, yes. And no, I did not purposely trigger a slide because he wasn't caving with me."

I heave another a big breath. No matter how often I try to explain the incident, Mica convinces others I am lying. So why bother to defend myself yet again? Because Ana hasn't been in Mica's sphere of influence long enough to have her opinion turned cement-hard against me. Maybe. And because once in a while, my need to state my innocence bursts out like an underground stream flooding into the light.

"Well," says Erin, leaning in close, her face and tone warm. "Some of us have never questioned that." Then she turns to Ana. "I like your costume, girl. Nice fangs, but careful not to get your tail stepped on."

"Thanks," Ana replies uncertainly, raising a tiger eyebrow.

No surprise that Erin, the alternative-vegan-environmentalist-leftie of the school, might be wary of Ana, the Big Boss's daughter who resembles a glamour model. Not that anyone has gotten to know Ana yet. A goal I intend to pursue. All I've heard is that her mom left her dad years ago and is not in touch. That would be a drag, especially since like me, she's an only.

"So, Hudson. Where's your costume?" Ana asks, clutching her beer can like it's an important prop.

"Oh, I'm not staying long enough to make one worth it," I say as I spot Don and Dirk catch sight of me and deliver evil eyes. "But how are you?" I'm trying to maintain the nerve to smile and look into her eyes at the same time.

Meanwhile Erin slips away, back into phantom mode.

"Mica has been showing off his limp like he's some kind of war hero. You guys had another incident in a cave?"

I sigh. "Yes, an incident. But no one was seriously hurt or traumatized. And a word to the wise: Don't believe everything you hear at Tass High."

"Of course not," she says, one tiger ear drooping. "Gutsy of you to give that talk at the community centre." The tone is neutral, neither approving nor disapproving. Again, I respect that she's practised at not revealing her cards, not showing interest in any one particular guy. She has probably always had her pick, I figure, so it's only natural she'd develop a wariness around guys who are all but falling at her feet. "You know a lot about caving."

"Caving is what I love. As do you, yes?" I say, moving slightly closer, enjoying a whiff of the jasmine and the thickness of her eyelashes over green eyes I want to swim in.

"It's tough getting up in front of a whole roomful of adults like that, on any topic," she dodges my question carefully, "though maybe easier when you're not new like me. Anyway, great presentation."

"Thanks. Went better than at school." *Thanks to no flying erasers.*

She laughs lightly, leaning toward me, which sends heat waves through my body. "The whipped cream!" Now she's bent over laughing, prompting me to do the same. Finally, she straightens up. "Tell me about some good hikes out of Tass, since I can't cave anymore."

"Can't or won't? Because if you want, we could hike up to—"

"Hudson!" Mica's use of my actual name and his pasted-on smile as he glides into our space must be due to the presence of a certain girl. "So sorry about your dad calling just now and saying you have to go home immediately. I never like to be the bearer of bad news." He winks at Ana, whose eyes narrow at that, and lays a firm hand on my shoulder to steer me out. "But you're looking good, man. Hope it's all hanging well for you."

"It's hanging—they're hanging—Mica, what are those guys doing? We need to stop them!" I point to the rear of the patio, where three guys have fumbled to the top of the two-storey rock wall and are clinging by their fingertips over the paving stones, attempting to scramble onward and upward. That puts them where dirt and roots replace rock, about one-third of the way to the clifftop above. Not even sober do they have a chance of ascending the rest of the way, especially with a chanting group below splashing water from the pool up at them, turning the dirt into mud.

"An accident waiting to happen," Ana says, one paw lifted to her mouth. "Mica? Hudson? You know them. Do something!"

"Guys! Stop it! Come down right now!" Mica shouts, moving toward them. But he stumbles, trips over the edge of the pool, and plunges in. That increases the merriment.

"Harry! Buzz! Larry!" I shout, hurrying over. "Seriously not cool! Hey, everyone, throw those cushions over there in case they fall." I point to the floral padding on the deck chairs. Erin and Ana leap to the task while others jeer me and cheer on the would-be cliff climbers. The three guys are well above the rockface now, laughing uproariously, pulling themselves up by stringy roots and jamming their fists into clumps of dirt that start raining down on the spectators. Mica has emerged from the pool and is shaking himself off like a wet dog.

"Move back!" I warn, pushing people away from the cushions.

That's when it happens—as it did to Mica and me what seems a lifetime ago. The dirt starts sliding, a portion of the cliff is collapsing, dirt and rocks rain down on the cushions, and three bodies, one at a time, fall hard on the prepared landing. Meanwhile, onlookers behind them stumble and fall backwards into the pool with cans of beer still clutched in their hands.

Mica steps into the melee to assess injuries. Erin grabs a first-aid kit from Mica's house and is doing rounds like Florence Nightingale. But somehow, none of the three drunk daredevils fell onto the patio stones, which could have resulted in serious injury. There are just a few minor scrapes and bruises, which Erin is bandaging. Ana stands in the shadows of the house's eaves, looking as unimpressed as an adult viewing misbehaving children. Cords twang in my neck. Does she think she's too good for the Tass student body?

The failed climbers glance about, looking stunned and embarrassed, then cover for that by shaking fists at the cliff and rolling about on the deck-chair cushions, laughing like hyenas.

"You can leave now," says a low, threatening voice so close to my neck that I feel the heat of his breath.

"Dirk," I say placidly, half turning around.

"What part of *now* do you not understand?" He puts his face right into mine, a bouncer who takes his job seriously. An arm grabs mine and thrusts me toward the patio entry gate.

Underground, Dirk's bulk is a hazard, an inconvenience. Up top, though, he rules over the likes of runts like me. No one's looking our way. I could mumble something about a free world, about the need to chill. But the highlight of the evening has played out. I came, I saw, I conversed with three-plus people, and I prevented another near death, even if the telling of events will be twisted by the golden gang once again. Time to move on.

I stroll away from the house as darkness closes in and am across and down the street when a police siren comes screaming past me. Uh-oh. A neighbour must have called the police.

Classmates stampede for the gate, but the police officers are too quick for them, hustling them back in. I see Mica being escorted to the centre of the patio, and I feel a stab of guilt for having escaped. Then again, it was a party to which I wasn't even invited. Mica turns and our eyes meet. I could swear there's a trace of wanting to say thank you, a mutual understanding that I had helped prevent a disaster. Maybe even a desire to apologize for how things went down in the cave the other day?

I miss Mica, comes into my head. *Does he ever miss me?* We were perfect caving partners. Overwhelming sadness descends on me, makes me sink down, cover my head, and punch a hole in the perfectly trimmed hedge beside me.

CHAPTER TWELVE

"Enjoy the party last night?" Mom asks, poking her head into my room the next morning.

I sit up, survey clothing scattered across the floor, and register that Mom is in her work clothes.

"I've left a list of chores for you on the kitchen counter. Dad has left already. I'm off to work now. The inspector is arriving at the office shortly."

"Will Dad get to talk to the guy?" I ask groggily.

"Woman, not guy," Mom says. "He might. We'll all catch up at dinner tonight, okay?"

"What's her name?" It occurs to me I could Google her credentials.

"Sandra Mast. Bye, honey."

I'm way too old to be called *honey.* Happy-happy family? I guffaw aloud at Erin's sense of humour and wish I'd had more time to talk with her at the party. I hope she didn't get into trouble there. Not that she was drinking beer, now that I think about it.

After Mom leaves, I try to get back to sleep but give up. I shower, toss on some clothes, and start up my laptop.

This Sandra Mast, it turns out, is not just a registered cave inspector who gets lousy reviews. She was also the official who founded the super-lucrative Little Caves enterprise near Campbell River. After a couple of local kids found the impressive series of grottos, she stickhandled all the paperwork to make it a profitable commercial cave business, in return for being part owner. Little Caves draws lineups of tourists every summer and employs a handful of full-time guides, the lucky things. Which means she'd know how to turn Mica, Jett, and me into millionaires if we locate the Castle-Dungeon connection. Well, okay, not millionaires. But it'd be fun.

Wait, what am I saying, *Mica*, Jett, and me?

Must find a way to talk with this Sandra Mast.

I eat breakfast, check off a few of Mom's chores, and bike to the school's basketball court, where kids hang out all summer long. On the way, I spot Mica chatting energetically with D-squared. Did he Google Ms. Mast too? Will his dad pull strings to get him in to see her? Is he going to promote what used to be *our* project: the connection, the secret Door?

I play basketball till lunchtime, then slip home to make a sandwich and carry it down to the riverbank. At the sound of lighthearted conversation and a woman's twittering laughter, I slide off my stump and stand behind a tree. Approaching just down the gravel path is Mr. Toop and a woman who's a dead ringer for the photo I saw on Google this morning: the one-star inspector. My big opportunity? Nope. No way can I step into her path with the VP there, and anyway, my instincts tell me to stay hidden. Something about how close the two are walking together, and the friendly, animated way they're conversing, tells me this is not a business twosome who just met this morning. It's altogether too cozy for an arm's-length inspector job. So, he's hired an acquaintance to rubber stamp whatever TT is doing. At least, that's my theory.

After they pass by, I finish my lunch and wander up to TT headquarters, a modest building overlooking the parking-lot-turned-crater.

"Well, hello, Hudson. Haven't you shot up this year?" exclaims the office's perky executive secretary, Trina Phelps.

"Um, thanks, Mrs. Phelps," I say awkwardly, heading toward Mom's small office, across from the front door.

"Hudson?" Mom says in surprise. "Are you okay?"

"I'm fine, Mom. Hey, can you get me an appointment with Ms. Mast? To talk about caves and stuff?"

Mom's hands rest on files spread across her desk. "Hudson, you know I can't do that. I'm just the bookkeeper, and she's tied up with execs and community leaders all day. She's not here to... Even your dad hasn't been able to..."

"Dad didn't bring his maps to show her, did he?"

"What maps would those be, young man?" comes a woman's voice. Mr. Toop and Ms. Mast have stepped through the front door.

Mom winces. Mr. Toop's eyes are lasering holes into my body as I whirl around and face them.

"Um, Mr. Toop, Ms. Mast, this is my son, Hudson. He's just dropping in for a quick visit."

"How nice," Ms. Mast says, looking me up and down. Her dyed-blond hair is wound into a bun at the back of her neck, and with her grey business suit and high heels, she doesn't look like she's planning to crawl around in a cave anytime soon. "I understand your father is a noted caver around these parts, in addition to being a long-time TT driver. He has some caving maps of the immediate region, does he? Because when we asked him this morning, he said he just uses what's publicly available."

I have a stab of panic before I think, *good old Dad.* "Um, yeah. That's what we use."

"Mrs., um, Gear," Mr. Toop addresses my mother.

"Greer," she corrects him politely.

"Can Ms. Mast and I borrow your son for a short conference in my office, please?"

"Of course!" Mom says, a little too brightly.

I follow the two into Mr. Toop's plush office next door to Mom's and sit stiffly in a leather guest chair pulled up to the chestnut desk. Pretty nice digs for someone who's been in Tass for such a short time. And he doesn't even know his bookkeeper's name. Ms. Mast eases herself down behind the desk in Mr. Toop's chair like she owns it. I should be delighted to get my "interview" with Ms. Mast, but somehow, I feel like I'm in the principal's office instead.

"I'll leave you two to it," Mr. Toop says, throwing me a squint-eyed look and closing the panelled door quietly behind him. Through the glass wall, I see him wander toward the coffee room.

"So, a fellow caver," Ms. Mast says, friendliness poured on like an over-application of perfume. "I presume you and Mica Brown know each other?"

I nod, since words have left me.

"He told me all about the Castle and the Dungeon—such clever names, you two! Very marketable. And he said you and your father have some maps that could be useful in my investigation."

Grrr.

"And the plan to find a join and open a mega-cave to the public. I love such ambition in young people! I've got lots of contacts and know-how if you do pull off such a feat and get Parks Canada approval. Assuming we could get TT on board, of course."

"Um, thanks."

"But—"

There had to be a "but."

"If you have maps of the passages beneath Tass's operation that would complement the LIDAR images I have to work with already"—she unlocks her briefcase and pulls out some kind of topographical documents—"that would help me ensure that your community stays safe, given that TT has agreed to adhere to specifications in my forthcoming report."

I know that LIDAR, which stands for "light detection and ranging," is a remote sensing method that calculates distance by bouncing laser light off an object. I swallow as she stares at me but refuse to be intimidated.

"May I look at what *you* have," I ask politely, "to see if what Dad and I have would add anything useful?"

"I'm sorry, Hudson. That would not be—" She looks up as the door opens.

It's Mom, who has probably heard every word spoken through the thin wall. "Ms. Mast, the GIS specialist you wanted to speak to is here. And he has just ten minutes before he has to be back on duty."

What does she mean by "on duty"? There's only one GIS specialist at TT, and he sits on his fat butt in the office the other side of Mom's all day long. He's certainly not important enough to dictate his availability to a visiting inspector.

"Of course, Mrs. Greer. Mica—er, Hudson—just give me a moment, okay?"

She stuffs the plan back in her briefcase, pushes on its clasp, rises from Mr. Toop's chair, and is out the door before I can respond. Mom retreats with a meaningful look, pulling the door almost closed.

Moving fast, I pull Ms. Mast's briefcase into my lap and nudge the clasp. It didn't lock! I yank the folds of paper out and scan them. Grabbing my phone from my pocket and holding the plans low between my legs, I start snapping, all but leaping into the air when the door hinges creak. But it's only a stray breeze. I complete my criminal act and stuff the plans back into the briefcase—pushing the clasp firmly enough to lock it this time—and place the briefcase back on her seat before Ms. Mast steps back in.

"The thing is, Ms. Mast, my dad and I, we just mess around a little underground. We're not professional cavers like you. And our maps are what you could buy anywhere, plus the equivalent of a few pencil scribbles on a napkin, as I'm sure Dad told you already." I rise, shrug nonchalantly, and head for the door. "There's nothing we have that could possibly help you." *Not that we would if we could.* "But welcome to Tass, good luck, and we're all very happy that TT is working with a top inspector like yourself."

I step out, wave at Mom, and march home. Did Mom actually wink at me? Is she protecting Dad and his maps, some of which even I've never seen? Has she read too many spy novels?

Light-footed now, I'm heading for Jett's house to tell him we're now that much closer to finding the secret Door.

It'll be a lively dinner at home tonight when I show Dad what we've got now to integrate with our sterling stash of maps. Our drafts are so professional, I realize now, that Ms. Mast would probably break a high heel to get her hands on them.

CHAPTER THIRTEEN

"I'm not sure about this inspector," Dad says to Mom, me, and Jett at lunch one day.

"In what way?" I ask, noting Mom pursing her lips like she has heard this before.

"I worry she's not objective, doesn't really have our community's safety front of mind, is perhaps going to rubber-stamp whatever TT wants."

"Honey, don't," Mom interrupts.

"Okay, never mind. Let's hope she's fine. But I've been talking to Mr. Williams, and he has the same concerns."

"Hmm," I say, not really wanting to get into it, not with caving maps in front of us and caving dreams to pursue.

For days now, Dad, Jett, and I have spent our evenings with heads bent over maps on the dining room table, while Mom keeps us fuelled with coffee and homemade cinnamon buns. Dad has all but emptied his precious safe of maps that, placed beside one another and thoroughly updated based on my snaps of TT's LIDAR file layers, give us a wealth of detail and exciting new exploration goals.

"What have you not explored around here?" I tease Dad.

"Oh, there's still plenty of Tass's underground to map," he replies. "For instance, according to what I see on this LIDAR document, there might be a route off a cave we gave up on a couple of years ago, way up in the northwest quadrant." He's got one finger on a yellowed hand-drawn map, and one on Ms. Mast's. "Or here, right near Ribbon Falls, there's a strong possibility of a passage. Again, how could we have missed that?"

"Because we don't have TT's fancy instruments and tools," Jett suggests. "Like, we've never hired a drone with satellite imagery capability or LIDAR."

"And we don't have their incentive to expand operations any which way they can," Dad grumbles.

"What about right here, in town?" I ask. "See that depression on the TT map? There's the slightest hint of grey under the community centre, too."

"Definitely not a go," Dad says, examining it under a magnifying glass and shaking his head. "But the northwest quadrant, that's got big potential."

I love the way he says it. So firmly, so certain. "Then I say let's look for an entrance up there!"

"It's private property," Mom says, reminding us she's in the room. "As in, TT's."

"Like that has ever stopped us," I say.

Dad, Jett, and I look at one another.

"This weekend!" Dad says with a determined grin.

Mom shakes her head and sighs. Dad turns sparkling eyes on her and rises to draw her into a happy-happy hug and jig that's totally embarrassing.

The next day, news has hit the student body that Mr. Williams has resigned. No! I'd hoped he'd change his mind.

That weekend, I walk over to his house after breakfast, hoping I'm not out of line. It's kind of invading his privacy, but he hasn't answered any of my phone calls. I need to submit my science-fair entry form, which requires his signature. An entry form he was supposed to help me fill out days ago. It takes a couple of buzzes for anyone to answer. Mr. Williams finally opens the door. He gives me a warm smile.

"Is this about the science-fair project, Hudson?"

"Um, yeah. Deadline is coming up, and I kind of need your autograph."

He squares his shoulders and opens the door wider. "Yeah, come in. Sorry about the mess. Wife and kids are at the in-laws for a few days."

Mess? It's as neat as if a team of cleaners and inspectors had just been around. Okay, there's a pack of unopened diapers on a counter, and some toddler toys in one corner, but everything is spotless and organized. A white lab coat hangs on a hook beside cooks' aprons. Rows of bookshelves hold tomes lined up according to topic: chemistry, physics, biology, environmental science. Chemistry sets sit on high shelves well out of children's reach.

A corner of the kitchen boasts sparkling-clean lab equipment, from glass beakers to a pH meter, a shiny new filing cabinet so full of files it bulges a little open. And in place of pride on the living room wall, where you might expect a nice picture to hang, is a giant topographic map of the Tass region. There are blue and red pencil marks all over it. Definitely a scientist's house. I catch him glancing at an unopened set of large new test tubes in his mini-lab.

"Still testing water purity?" I ask.

He nods vigorously. "I have more time to do that now."

"Will you ever come back to Tass High? What's up?"

"Can't say, Hudson." His eyes glow with energy like he's a man with an exciting secret. "All in good time. Sorry," he adds as an afterthought. "Hey Hudson, in your caving explorations, have you ever been in this area?" He points to the northwest quadrant of upper Castle terrain, way upstream of Ribbon Falls. It's exactly where Dad, Jett, and I plan to scout today, based on our new conglomeration of TT and Dad's maps.

"Nope. Why?"

"Oh, I heard a rumour there's a nice hot spring up there. Thought it might be somewhere I could take my wife and kids on a little hike."

"Even though it's TT land?"

He winks. "Isn't everything around here?"

I'm still studying the map. He has outlined all the creeks with a bright blue marker and circled various places in red. I glance at the lab equipment again, and the black box on a high shelf that spilled during our last conversation. Maybe not such a weird hobby for a science guy. And it's none of my business how he plans to support his family without teaching at Tass High.

"Hey, let's get out of this stuffy house and sit outside," he says.

I follow him out the door to a wooden bench by his backyard garden full of ripening vegetables. We sit in silence for a moment while I watch ants swarm over a sizeable anthill in front of us.

"There was an inspector in town," I tell him. "She's supposed to make sure TT isn't over-felling trees or building roads where they aren't safe. I asked my mom to suggest to her that she check out the community centre building and property."

He flicks an ant off his jeans leg. "Token inspector, works for the Dark Side, is getting double pay is my guess," comes the firm response.

I brush three ants off my arm. Okay, for sure Mr. Williams has never hidden his distrust of the company. He was pretty much using me to get up their nose at that meeting, as I kind of knew even at the time. But whatever's going on, he's a good guy and a good teacher.

He keeps saying it was his decision to quit but I can't help imagining a rap on his knuckles from the principal, weak threats from TT, and pressure from his wife to stick to teaching. Even if his knowledge coupled with political pressure might save our town from the next sinkhole disaster.

An ant bites my ankle, so I lean down and pull up my socks. Maybe if I tell Mr. Williams about the inspector's maps I photographed, it will cheer him up. Maybe he could find info in there to pursue his not-so-secret campaign against TT's lack of environmental compliance. Dad and I are interested only in the caving secrets the material is revealing. But even as I open my mouth to spill about the maps, I shut it again. What I've done could get Dad and Mom fired. And how do I know that Mr. Williams's anti-TT attitude didn't get him fired from Tass High?

"No hot springs, Mr. Williams, or I'd know about it."

"The form," he says. "Where do I sign and when is it due?" He takes the paper I offer him.

"Friday." I'm taken aback he doesn't even remember the deadline. His mind is definitely on other things. Maybe he has a new job lined up? "Thanks again for letting me enter the fair."

He signs the sheet without even reading all the stuff he was supposed to fill in, which I winged. As he hands it back to me, I leap up and start brushing off all the ants that are on my body.

"Gross! Ouch!" Another ant bite. I'm so annoyed that I move to the anthill and plunge a heel into its dome.

"Hey, that's a sophisticated colony you're messing with," Mr. Williams objects.

I smile, then notice that he's not.

"An anthill is a complex structure full of tunnels and cavities the population builds cooperatively by continuously moving chunks of dirt four times their own body weight."

Ever the science teacher. I sit back down to put up with the rest of an ant lesson, not that I really mind.

"Ever heard about the former ant city a professor excavated in Brazil?" he asks.

"No. How do you excavate an anthill?"

"Researchers spent three days pouring ten tons of cement down the holes. When it hardened, it revealed an astounding metropolis of highways, chambers, fungus gardens, rubbish pits, and ventilated tunnels."

"Cool. Ants sound kind of smart, and they'd get along well with cavers."

He gives me a thumb's up. "The scientists calculated the ants had moved forty tons of soil to build it by doing millions of trips to the surface."

"No way. How big was this anthill?" I say, feeling a ping of guilt for denting his backyard anthill, but I'm also still flicking the insects off my clothes to avoid more bites.

"Three parking spaces wide, and the same depth as a city bus is long."

I hang my head exaggeratedly, but smirk. "Sorry I messed with this city, and maybe squished some citizens in the process."

"Picture a full crowd seated in a roofed stadium," Mr. Williams says.

I settle back on the bench to listen to Science Lesson No. 2. "Okay."

"The roof collapses. How do the spectators escape?"

I pinch an ant between a finger and thumb and fling him back to his subterranean superstructure. "The ones not crushed by dropping debris huddle in the middle or scramble for the exits, meaning the doorways on each level up and down the aisles that lead to the outer ring. You know, where the bathrooms and concession stands are."

"Exactly. That's what the ants you just messed with are doing." I smile.

He frowns. "That's what I picture the congregation doing during the big sinkhole here all those years ago."

A cloud hides the sun, causing a shadow to fall over the yard. "You mean some might have escaped from the fallen church into caves and tunnels? Not that it did them much good," I reflect dourly. "Maybe just delayed their death." I rise and take one last look at the damaged anthill, which is already being repaired rapidly by a team of super-excavators, and I scratch my ant bites, which maybe I deserve.

"Well, thanks for signing my form, Mr. Williams," I say as his gaze seems to drift off elsewhere. "See you around."

"Yup, see you around," he says, and walks to the house with a light gait, like he's a man with a mission.

CHAPTER FOURTEEN

"There aren't any hot springs above Ribbon Falls, are there?" I ask Dad and Jett as we make our way through tangles of salal the next day. It's what I told Mr. Williams, but I am doublechecking just in case Dad knows something I don't. We're farther northwest of town than we've ever caved, and my heart is beating hard at the anticipation of new underground explorations. Ms. Mast left town without further hassling Dad or me about maps, but she sure doesn't know what gems she left behind with us.

"Nope. Not a chance," says Dad. "Though there are some northeast of TT's property line. Your mother and I used to sneak in and enjoy them when we were young, before a landslide kind of wrecked them."

We pause to check the map and Dad's compass, then shove through thicker underbrush, scratchy plants tugging at our trousers. Pine tree branches extend bright green tips our way, as if showing off electric-green nail polish. It smells earthy and moist in the forest, and there's a hint of wild jasmine in the air. I love summer in the woods. Farther along, moss offers a soft carpet as we approach a house-high pile of boulders with ferns bursting out between them. There's a tinkle of running water and a scattering of osprey in the sky above us as we skirt the rocks. Soon we're following a crystal-clear creek of ancient beauty.

"Somewhere here is an entrance." Dad pauses and studies the map he has zipped into a protective plastic sheath.

But there's nothing obvious in our glade of fresh-smelling forest.

"Are you sure?" Jett asks, picking up a stick and poking about.

I follow the streamlet with my eyes until I spot a second micro-stream joining it. Leaping across the water, I tramp upstream through swampy ground until the wannabe-waterway disappears through a crack in a rock wall.

"Got it!" I call out, but as I duck under sturdy vines and feel around for a gap that might accept a size-small caver, I feel something sharp. "Ouch," I cry, withdrawing a hand bleeding from puncture wounds.

Moving the vines more cautiously, I see a dark triangle the size of a pup tent entryway that leads into damp darkness. Someone has fixed barbed wire across it. *What the—?*

Dad and Jett are on my heels in seconds. A cool breeze exhales into our faces from the depths of the cave as my fingers drip splotches of bright red onto the ferns.

"You okay, Huds?"

"Fine."

"Someone," Dad says in an ominous voice, "hiked all the way here carrying barbed wire and a portable, battery-powered, hammer-action drill and masonry bit. They attached bolts to each side of this entryway and strung up this nasty wire. For what? Who do they think is looking for what?"

Mica? I wonder. TT? Nah. Makes no sense at all.

We crouch and glance suspiciously about us as if anticipating hidden cameras, drones, or ninja-outfitted Special Forces.

Eventually, Dad slides his pack off his shoulders, unzips it, and pulls out some wire cutters. We've had to clip the lower wires of fences before to roll under them, but I didn't know he hauled them around on every hike.

"It's a cave, for heaven's sake," he says.

"I'm naming it Aladdin's Cave." I smile. "Gotta be full of jewels if someone went to this kind of trouble."

"Aladdin got the door slammed behind him after he ventured inside," Jett weighs in.

"Ha ha," I say.

"Yeah, well, you two just keep on dreaming while I focus on furthering the cause of cartography," Dad says. His clippers snap one, then another wire. Soon it's all clear. We dig into our packs for headlamps and helmets. "Mind you don't catch yourself on those loose wires as you crawl in."

Past the entryway, the passages are damp and of a generous size as we splash up the feeder stream to ever-expanding rooms. Some formations look like bunches of carrots. Some mimic curtains. Some simulate popcorn. In one chamber, Dad shines his beam on a colony of bats, which resemble a throbbing brown honeycomb.

A few flit down as if to inspect us, then do high-speed barrel rolls returning to home base, like small stunt-flying planes. Squeaks and squawks from their roosts fill our ears and make me want to duck my head, even though it's a myth that they go for human hair.

"Maternity ward in winter, but male bats are allowed in here at the moment because it's past that season," Dad whispers, as if the bats might be offended by voices. "But we still need to pass through quickly, leave them in peace."

"They're really picky about airflow," I add, remembering Ana's comment in class, and also what a guide said when Mom, Dad, and I visited Kartchner Caverns State Park in Arizona. "They need a really constant temperature and humidity level to establish a stable hibernaculum for calving." I love using the right words for the place they hibernate and give birth.

"Bats *calve*?" Jett guffaws. "Who'd have thought?"

I can't help wondering what will happen to colonies like this if these caves ever open up to guided tours. Maybe some batty citizen wired the entrance shut to help protect the colony? I remember how the Kartchner guide said tours didn't run in that area during times when the mothers needed quiet, and how the guides used the tour to educate the public about bats. In fact, the rancher who owned the land was persuaded to let the cave go commercial only because he was a former science teacher who understood the cave's educational value.

That's what our Tass caves will do! Educate misguided, power-hungry people like Mr. Toop.

At one point the rocky tube we're in stretches downward like a serpent-carved spiral staircase, leading to—well, somewhere. I imagine it delivering us to a thunderous waterfall, a cathedral of scalloped marble, or a turquoise pond that has never seen light. Then again, it might lead to nothing more than a dead-end mud boulevard. It's impossible to know until we get there. Not knowing is half the thrill. Even better, the smooth mud floor proves no one has ever planted their feet here before.

After two hours of scrambling from one passage to another, helping each other up steep ramps and scraping our shoulders and helmets in caterpillar tunnels, we find ourselves gazing in awe at a lone cathedral room filled with sparkling stalagmites and stalactites. Finding a smooth, flat place to lie down, I gaze up in wonder, headlamp making the ceiling glisten as if we're in a planetarium.

I see small and large stalactites; mineral layers that hang down from the ceiling like a cow's udders; soda straws, thin-walled hollow tubes that look like skinny stalactites; stalagmites, which grow up from the floor like carrots, pointy tip up; impressive columns that look like they belong in a Greek temple. To my left I see the aptly named cave grapes, and then there are my favourite formations of all: "draperies," sheets of slow-flowing calcium carbonate that look like elegant floor-to-ceiling curtains. And as if to pretty up the place, there are cave pearls.

Each of these treasures takes thousands of years to grow. I remember being angry when I heard a story about how some English yahoos in the 1800s went into a cave with precious stalactites the height of human beings, and for "fun," shot them down one by one with a hunting rifle.

There's also a bacon-strip formation that looks exactly like its name, with alternating dark and light bands. All this cave seems to be missing are the fountain-like formations called rimstone dams, and flowstone, which resembles wax flowing all over the walls and floors.

"I could happily fall asleep here," I say.

"Me too," Jett says, flopping down beside me.

"We've pulled off another one," I announce, squaring my shoulders. "Can't wait till we open up tours and share this with the world."

Dad finds a boulder seat and takes out pad and paper to make notes about what we've found.

"It's a beauty," he agrees.

Fifteen minutes later, after we've scrambled to our feet and explored onward, it's my turn leading and I halt at a fork.

"Hmm, which way, Cartographer? There seems to be an Aladdin II down here." I hear the crinkle of paper as Dad studies his notes. He's in his element, exploring new territory and expanding his maps. It's a toss-up who'd be greener with envy if they could see him now: Mica or Ms. Mast. But neither will lay a finger on our hard work anytime soon—Mica because he chose to go rogue, to terminate our friendship, and Ms. Mast because Dad and Mr. Williams think she's only masquerading as an inspector who's ensuring our community's safety.

"My guess," Dad says with a tremble of excitement in his voice, "is that one of these two routes leads to something great."

"And the other," Jett adds, "is going to plunge down to a hellish dead-end mudhole with a fire-breathing dragon kept there by TT. So we'd better choose carefully."

Dad grins and speaks.

> *"Two roads diverged in a cave, and I—*
> *I took the one less travelled by,*
> *And that has made all the difference."*

"I'm pretty sure Robert Frost wasn't a caver," I say. "No pressure, but which one?"

Jett makes like a sniffer dog. "What does the secret Door smell like?"

Dad rolls his eyes. I fist-bump Jett as we study our fearless leader. Dad leans his face into one passage, then the other, turning his cheek as if waiting for a kiss. What he is doing, of course, is waiting for his cheek to feel air current. Which passage has a wisp of air current, the indication of a possible exit? I lean this way and that to duplicate his efforts. My judgment says the left one.

Dad smiles and jerks his head to the right. We stumble after him without arguing. Another forty-five minutes of rock above, beneath, and around us. Cold, hard cocoons endlessly beckoning us to crawl just a little farther. Rock passages we've never traversed before, slowly and gradually being added to Dad's master plan. Passages that march into darkness, twisting, shrinking, and expanding around us.

"Once we get to the Castle-Dungeon join, I sure hope it won't be far to an exit," I grumble. "'Cause I've kind of had it for the day, and Mom's going to start worrying. We've been in here way longer than we planned."

"You're young and strong, at the peak of your fitness, son. If I can do it, you two can. Just follow the air current. We're coming close already, I'd say."

"I smell grass and hear birds," Jett states.

My senses also tell me the beckoning finger of air movement we've been following all along is tinged with an outdoor smell now. Dirt, grass, cedar. Like sea-weary sailors who sight land, we sense freedom is at hand. My elbows and knees would worship a meadow right now.

The thought has barely registered when Dad holds up a hand. As if we need a signal to stop and listen to a new sound: a low rumbling far ahead. Not a rockfall or earthquake type of groan. More like a small motor. A dirt mover. A Cat! There's a screech of metal on stone that makes my heart beat harder, and a thump and tremor that moves from the cave floor through our knees. Then comes the whine of a giant mosquito. Or chainsaw.

"Logging and roadwork crew?" says Dad. "But we shouldn't be anywhere near a TT project."

"Do you know every TT project going on?" Jett asks.

Dad goes quiet. "I used to. But lately the execs are stingier with what info they share even with us long-timers."

I breathe in deeply, if only to steady my nerves, and nearly choke on a lungful of dust floating toward us. We're clearly near an exit, which means today's not our day for finding the elusive connecting passage. But it does mean we'll be out soon. Hopefully not within sight of whoever's working, given it would be TT land.

"No big deal. We can keep our heads down, or say we've been hiking and got lost," I say.

Dad frowns. "We especially need to keep out of sight if there's unsanctioned activity going on."

Jett takes over the lead. The noise grows louder as a shaft of light comes into view. It's not the wide beam of light I expect from an exit, more like a thin laser beam. It backlights endless dust particles floating in the air. Meanwhile, the breath of fresh air laced with the scent of greenery is gone, reduced to nostril-clogging dust and a whiff of gasoline.

"An exit, yes!" Jett exclaims, then halts. "Nooo!"

"What?" I ask from just behind him.

"Barbed wire."

I hear Dad swear under his breath, then he speaks loudly enough for the rest of us to hear. "We'll just use the wire cutters again."

"Barbed wire *and* a boulder rolled up against it." Jett enunciates each word as if daring the news to echo.

That's when it occurs to me that the sound of the Cat is moving away. It's already almost inaudible. The floor vibrations are gone. The machine was here, very close by. Now it's headed away.

Dad has moved his face to the crack between the cave wall and boulder blockade. "I see chainsaws and a cable skidder, TT logo on them. Stacks of logs and tons of slash. They're clear-cutting this patch and putting in a road as they go, despite it being beside a creek, which is strictly against regulations. I know exactly where this is. TT would never have gotten permission. It's remote enough they figure they can get away with it, especially with only a handful of vehicles and probably a selection of workers paid a bonus to keep their mouths shut. Interesting that I've never been informed of this operation." The last bit comes out in an ominous tone.

Is it my imagination, or are there shouts and whistles out there? "Dad, something's going on."

He and Jett peek through the gap and then turn to me with widened eyes.

"A machine has skidded into the ditch," Dad reports. "And from there into the stream. That'll cost them, and silt up the town's water. At least we have something entertaining to watch for a while. Boys, we need a break. Time to eat our sandwiches."

We're munching away, gobbling down PB&Js and homemade granola bars and discussing what to do, when a new sound reaches our ears: the rigorous clanging of a faraway bell.

"The firehall bell!" Jett says.

An emergency!

I see Dad shudder before he presses his face so hard against the crack that he's going to end up with a welt. "Landslide, I'm thinking," he says. "That rig that slid off the road has probably blocked the water and triggered landslides downstream, closer to town. No danger to us, but the firehall obviously sighted them. Let's get out of here and see if we can help. Others will be coming up the hill, so they won't notice where we came from."

We explode into action, Dad rising to clip the wire, and all three of us pushing, pushing, pushing on the boulder in hopes of moving it enough for an escape slot. Jett cups his hands and tries shouting through the crack for help, but Dad says, "They'll never hear us, boys. They're down by the landslide. We have to push this boulder out on our own."

Never have I put more muscle into a shove. But our trio's huffing, puffing, and groaning isn't budging the giant blockade. A sense of claustrophobia descends. I fight off the tightness in my chest by beating on the slab till my knuckles bleed, and squeezing my eyelids shut to prevent tears from escaping. All the while, the shouts and the melancholy toll of the bell are messing with my nerves.

I shove my face against the small crack and look for any sign of people close enough to hear us. I'm trembling and sweat-soaked. No one. Wait! Movement on the far side of the new clearing. A man, moving about like he doesn't want to be seen, aiming something at the stumps and brush. Though he's too far away to hear us, the figure seems familiar. In fact, given what he's wearing, I'm certain it's Mr. Williams with a camera. Then he disappears in the hazy air, like nothing and no one was ever there.

"Dad, Jett, I see Mr. Williams out there."

"Close enough to hear us?" Dad asks.

"No."

Dad grips my wrists and pulls me away from the blockage, embraces me in a comforting hug. "Save your energy, boys. We have a three-hour crawl back to where we came in."

Retrace our entire crawl? My body slumps. It's what Mica had to do when my landslide mishap blocked his exit. His delusional resentment has affected my life since, but maybe particularly infested my karma today.

"They seem to have blocked this exit on purpose," Dad says. "I don't know why, but that's the way it is. And no matter who did it, we can't assume it was done with any knowledge that we were in here at the time."

Sweat drips down my forehead. *Be like Dad. Act like a leader. Keep the exhaustion out of your voice.*

"We're tough," I say. "We have the stamina to turn around, do the slog, and exit where we came in. Ready, team?"

CHAPTER FIFTEEN

Jett and I are lying full length on my bedroom floor, propped up on our elbows, staring at Ms. Mast's map with pencils poised to add details we recall from our last caving foray. It has been a few days since we escaped from Aladdin's Cave. Days in which the whole town has been under a boil-water advisory, given that the landslide clouded up the town's small reservoir. It's a total pain, and everyone has been saying Mr. Williams is flitting about the forest taking water samples like some kind of hyped-up hummingbird and lecturing anyone within earshot that TT is fouling up some of the purest water on the West Coast.

Dad made some quiet inquiries of workmates to confirm that TT is taking down trees and building a new road along the stream near Aladdin—approved by the rubber-stamp inspector, of course. TT execs have taken no responsibility for the boil-water order or landslide, just said it's "under investigation" and "there's no proven connection with logging operations." Meanwhile, they have ordered in a truckload of bottled water for employees.

For a week now, Dad has been pressed to put in serious overtime, so Jett and I are spending all our spare time huddled over any maps Dad hasn't shoved back into his safe.

"Hey, look at this old map with empty white spaces where your dad never got around to exploring. Is that his handwriting?"

I laugh. "Yes, he's written 'Here be dragons.' He told me it's an actual line from a famous globe created in 1504." Then I sigh. "I'm dying to go caving again, but I guess we need to wait for Dad's schedule to ease up."

"What's TT got your dad doing that makes him never around anymore?" Jett asks.

"Repairs. Haven't you heard all that racket at the community centre lately?"

"Super noisy, for sure. They're fixing the foundation or something?"

"Pouring grout into all the little cracks that have opened up in recent months. Even though Dad told them it will only make it look better, not actually stabilize it. In fact, sometimes grout-fills can cause sinkholes."

"Sounds about right." Jett grimaces. "Now, about this map."

Jett and I have sketched Aladdin's Cave in as much detail as we can and are eager to explore Aladdin II—the fork we didn't take that day with Dad. But as my buddy and I stare at Ms. Mast's map, my finger keeps returning to a vague shading. The possible hollow on the map is right in town, a long way downhill of Aladdin. It's almost like my hand is being drawn to a spot on a Ouija Board.

To me, it seems to indicate a cave that none of our older maps do, in an area we've never found access to explore. But Dad is way better at reading geological data than me and has shown no interest, so I'm clearly wrong. Or am I?

"Absolutely nothing there," he insisted when Jett and I pointed it out. "Just a smudge on the map. Trust me."

"Why is Dad so sure it's a no-go, do you think?" I ask Jett now. He cranes his neck to take it in, then examines the older maps. "Dunno, but it's not on any of his other maps, and he definitely said not to bother with it. Whereas he's totally excited about the northwest quadrant."

"Mmm. Want to go wander around town over that shadow area anyway?"

Jett's eyebrows bunch up. "Rule of Three."

"I didn't say actually go in if we find an entrance. Just poke around, you know?"

"We should definitely wait for your dad."

"But he's always working. And he doesn't think anything is there. Just this once, you and me?"

Jett shrugs like he knows he has lost already. My spine tingles as I leap up and grab my caving pack, tossing in a second helmet for Jett in case the two of us decide to crawl in… just a little way. Jett notices and shakes his head, but he follows me downstairs, where we leave a note for my mom.

"At least we're not trespassing this time," I say.

"Yeah, instead of TT land, it's the centre of town," he grouses. "It'll be all cockroaches and garbage."

I kick a rusty can down pot-holed Main Street in front of us and pause to appreciate afternoon sunlight glinting off the stained glass of our church, the one that replaced the sunken one lost so long ago. Definitely not as pretty as Dad's model church. Over the years, I've clued in that he gets quiet and sad every time he passes the new church. He must still carry trauma from the Big One.

Jett and I walk our little town like we're rescuers doing a grid search for a lost child. Up and down, back and forth, checking everything from mossy basement corners to bursts of ferns in the park. We step purposefully on any soft, damp spots that might be mushy enough to sink our shoe tips into a hidden hole.

We've pretty much covered every inch of the place in an hour and are heading to the gas station for a soda when I spot Ana. She's alone except for a Saint Bernard on a leash.

"Hey, Ana!" She's wearing shorts and a black tank top that show off a deep tan, a model's legs, and firm arms.

I veer over to her before Jett can interfere. "Nice dog. What's his name?"

"Trog."

"Trog? Short for Troglodyte, meaning cave dweller?" I grin and pat its head. The dog's pink tongue lolls out and friendly eyes blink at me as it nudges its head into my thigh, almost knocking me over. "Whoa, he must weigh about the same as me!"

"Pretty much," she says, smiling.

"Does he cave?" I joke.

"He's actually crazy about caves. Sniffs them out like normal dogs go for rabbit holes. I'm forever having to pull him out of them." She feeds him a treat from her pocket. "Hey, what are you two up to? Searching for lost treasure? Or caving," she says, pointing to the helmet bulges in my pack. "No, not caving, because there are only two of you."

"Just hanging out, Ana. And there are only two of us 'cause your dad makes mine do so much overtime," I joke, wanting to kick myself after the words are out of my mouth. "But wait, *now* there are three of us," I say brightly.

"Three for a soft drink at the gas station maybe," she tosses back.

Is she flirting with me? I turn my reddening face to Jett, who's shaking his head.

"Not me," he says to her. "I'm busy checking out a new caving lead, with or without this bum. And the first one who finds it gets to name the discovery." He knows my favourite part of caving is naming new chambers. He's also being nice enough to give me one-on-one time with my crush.

"Like where?" Ana asks.

"Actually, we could use a drink," I say. "You can join us, Jett," I add, needing his presence to help steel my nerves. He doesn't object. I lean down to give Trog a sort-of hug. Showing fondness for their dogs is always the way to a girl's heart, right? But the beast trots off to a side street to sniff a manhole cover, then pee on it.

Okay, whatever. Wait, cave-sniffing dog? And manhole cover! Why hasn't that made it onto our radar before now? I stare at the rusty old circle off Main Street like I haven't passed by it and over it millions of times before. I also notice it has been cemented closed, but the cement has gradually worn away.

Like it has some kind of pull on me, I walk over and ease Trog to one side, place my hand on its handle, and attempt a lift. The cast-iron lid is stuck solidly, of course.

"Eww," Jett says. "The dog just peed there."

But Ana's faster than Jett on the uptake. "Nooo. Tell me you're not going down a sewer hole to try and find a cave entrance." Her face is crinkled with concern, or maybe it's curiosity.

I know I should move away and immediately lob a funny line back at her, say something about her dog, or in some other way mislead her as to my impulsive intentions. But Jett has dropped everything, walked over, bent down, and put his own muscle into moving the heavy lid. Next thing I know, Ana and I are side-by-side helping him. Good that we're off Main Street, not easily visible to traffic.

Even so, a car that has turned up the street blasts its horn and the grizzled driver veers around the three of us, shouting, "Get out of the road, you idiots!"

"Hold on," Ana says and heads back to Main and into the

gas station. She returns holding a crowbar. Fitting it into a small hole, she pops the lid like she's peeling back the tab on a beer. So much for the long-ago cement job. We all lean down.

Trog is licking his owner's face, Ana is trying to get a tighter hold on his leash, and Jett and I already have our heads and shoulders well into the hole.

"Feel that breeze," Ana says softly, her face suddenly beside mine, making me catch my breath. "Since when do sewer lines have a strong uplift draft that doesn't even smell like—like sewage? Maybe your hunch was right, Hudson."

She's definitely a caver in her bones, even if trying to be an ex-caver.

The four of us, Trog included, kneel around the circle heedless of the traffic down on Main, which involves one dented pickup truck in the ten minutes we sit there like stunned stooges. Iron rungs form a ladder down the dark chimney. Footholds to a passage to a maze to the Door, I just know it. Wait till I tell Dad.

I straighten up and look around for anyone staring at us. Nobody. With monumental effort, I drag the lid back on, clap the filth off my hands, and stand.

"Cavers, time to retreat to a private bench at Tass Gas and not draw attention to ourselves, don't you agree?" I ask. "Trog, thank you for giving us the idea. Ana, are you interested in joining a top-secret mission, or are you capable of pretending that none of what just happened, happened?"

She scratches Trog's head, looks from Jett and me to the manhole, and rules, "At heart I guess I'm still a caver. How would I be able to resist the idea of a top-secret mission? As long as you're not going to tell my dad."

I breathe a sigh of relief. "No worries there."

Jett speaks up. "I'm so hungry, I gotta eat something now, before we go down that hole."

"Then we'll just take a quick fifteen," I say, "and plan it out while we're eating."

Soda and pizza lead to ice cream and caving tales, which lead to all of us leaving messages on our parents' phones about being home late.

"Tell me about the geology of the Tass area," Ana says.

"Huh? Lots of limestone," I say, "which is one type of karst. Water erodes it easily, especially acidic rainwater. So, the water passes through the soil and enters the rock layer through cracks. It literally eats away the rock, makes it kind of brittle, and forms holes. That makes for cool caves, but also creates the danger of sinkholes."

"Got it," she says, a little impatiently. "But I've also heard there's molten granite up on the ridges." She waves her hand in the general direction of Aladdin's Cave, uphill of Ribbon Falls. "Dad, who's a geologist, says when magma hardens, it forms a crust over the granite and separates it from the limestone."

"Um, cool," I say, feeling outclassed and stupid. I change the subject. "Are you settling in, liking Tass better?"

She hesitates before going all animated. "Oh, totally liking it now," she enthuses. "Especially since meeting you guys." She's mostly looking at me. Her voice has gone soft, and her eyelashes flutter. My face heats up. Then she lobs a question out of left field. "So, do you and your dad have maps of the region around here? I'd be really into seeing them."

I flinch. Jett raises an eyebrow.

"We have the same maps anyone else has," I say in a tight voice.

She studies me carefully.

"Hey, guys, bathroom break. See you in a minute," Jett says.

This is my chance. I pull all my courage together. "Want to go to a movie sometime, Ana?"

She looks completely unsurprised, though not pleased in any obvious way.

"I'd like that, Hudson Greer," she says, as if we've just concluded a business deal. She reaches over and squeezes my hand while grinning at me. Wow! It was that easy? *Too easy*, some dumb, insecure part of me whispers.

We chat for a few moments, me sitting tall when Jett reappears. I'm tingling right to my toes. To hide my blush, I check my phone. Two calls from Mom. Well, I'm not returning them now. I feel kind of lousy tucking my phone back into my pocket, but Mom will understand when I explain our new find, or else Dad will convince her.

"No one can see us go down there," I say in a low voice, though the only person in the vicinity is a bored-looking, out-of-earshot gas station attendant sitting on a rusty chair behind the gas station, eyes glued to his phone.

"Rule of Three?" Ana questions, eyebrows knit. "I can't actually go down there. No gear, plus my dad would freak."

"With you as lookout, we're three," I assure her.

She hides a smile and nods. "Okay, I'll sit here with Trog and make sure a garbage truck doesn't park on the lid while you're exploring."

She seats herself on the curb, crowbar still in one hand, Trog's leash in the other. "Phone when you're finished and under the lid again, and I'll let you know when it's all clear to come out. If you're not back in one hour, I'll call 911."

I direct a grim smile her way. "Call my dad before you call 911. But we'll be back before then, I promise." Should I be crossing my fingers behind my back?

CHAPTER SIXTEEN

The steel handles are cold and moist in the dark confines of the chimney as I lower myself down, rung by rung, into the creepy blackness. Wind whistles around me, raising goosebumps on my arms. Guilt over doing this without Dad prickles my neck. But Ana's watchful presence up top counts for something. I feel more than see Jett's form above me, then hear the soft clank of the lid closing, and a good-luck bark from Trog.

"Committed," I whisper as I click my headlamp on.

"Are you sure we can wrestle that lid up when we want to come out?" Jett asks.

"Of course," I say casually. "Ana's there with a crowbar. She'll also make sure we don't get pancaked by a car as we pop up."

"That would be a crushing end to our endeavours." His voice sounds muffled in the tight space. "So, we are in some side leg of the Dungeon, correct?"

"Correct. Heading toward the Castle." One foot slips off the rung and nearly sends me down into the unknown. "This one's it, you know, Jett." My voice sounds hushed and reverent, even to me. "The portal, the hatch, the brass ring, ground zero. Dungeon, meet Castle. Castle, meet Dungeon. World, meet Tass."

Jett snorts. Then says under his breath, perhaps thinking I can't hear, "Mica should be here."

"Ow!" I say.

"What?"

"You stepped on my hand!"

"Then move along, Mr. Dreaming-in-Technicolour."

"I got a date with Ana," I announce triumphantly. "Sort of."

"Aha, that explains the neon glow coming off you when I returned. What were her terms, an hour with your dad's maps?"

I grind my teeth. "Back off, Jett."

"Okay, sorry. Way to go, Romeo."

Eventually the rungs end, and I drop onto firm dirt. "Tunnel," I call out with rising excitement. It's hunched-shoulders height. The tunnel echoes my words back at me in muffled form.

"And no water? No poop? No river of rats?"

I shiver. "No, Jett. I have a feeling it has been dry since before we were born. Tass's sewage must have been diverted elsewhere."

"Let's hope." He springs down beside me, and we shine our lights down a long, black corridor. For the first ten minutes of walking, it's an aged culvert with a gravelly floor whose rusty smell permeates our senses. Then the rippled metal ends in jagged edges, and a short while later, an ancient cave-in announces the end of the road. Except for a hole into a downward-slanted tunnel directly in front of the heap of rocks. I lean down and a breeze tickles my nose, which makes me smile.

I stick my head fully into the cave passage and start squirming forward. It's as claustrophobic as passages get. I'm one hundred percent certain that Dad's frame wouldn't allow him to enter it. Jett is going to be challenged. I can't even stick out my elbows. And it goes down, down, down, as dark, steep, and twisty as a black-hole waterpark slide. It's so tight, Jett and I won't be able to talk or hear each other.

Something wraps itself around my ankle and yanks, and I yelp. But it's Jett, complaining about my high-speed slithering. It's true I didn't consult with him before plunging into this wormhole. Three tugs would be a "stop right now" danger signal, but I consider one to be just a little whining on his part. He's right if he's thinking it's going to be a serious drag backing up all this distance if there's a dead end ahead with no turnaround space. Bad me. I smile, shake my foot from his grip, and keep going.

Rarely have I come across a passage that descends so fast. The rocky floor is still dry, but I'm half expecting to meet seawater at this rate. I picture coming nose-to-nose with a Tass Bay dolphin. But hallelujah, it finally levels out and grows slowly in volume until it reaches a mini-grotto in which Jett and I can pause, and we sit side-by-side with legs crossed like we're yogis.

"So," I say, wiping grit off my face, or more like smearing it around more.

"So," Jett echoes in a disgruntled voice. "We've been in here twenty minutes already. Another ten and we'll have to turn around if we don't want Ana to launch a search and rescue op."

I grin. "She won't do that. Maybe she'll come join us instead."

"Sure, or she'll send Trog in with a barrel of brandy 'round his neck." He rolls his eyes.

I point my light ahead of us. "Looks like it stays level for a while. With a little more room to scrabble around. And there's still air current coming our way. Can you smell water?"

Jett sniffs and shrugs.

Pulling out our maps, I make notes as I shiver in our dark little den.

"Where are we?" Jett asks, drawing a tic-tac-toe in the loose dirt beside us.

"In the Dungeon somewhere very near the Castle." I'm unable to keep a quiver of excitement out of my voice. "We've never gotten this close to the border, Jett."

"Stop kidding me."

"I'm not."

We sit silent for a moment, letting that sink in.

"What's on the surface above us?" Jett finally asks.

"The hill above town. The cemetery and public garden next to it." *The garden built over where the church sank.* Dad would tell us to back off and respect the dead.

We look at each other uneasily, then at the darkness ahead. Wind whistles over our heads like it's coming from the puckered lips of a ghoul.

I wet my finger and raise it. "Definitely still air current." I'm both relieved and puzzled. Will this passage lead to another sewer chimney, perhaps with its manhole cover off, thus letting all this air in? Or does the former sewer line run into a natural cave with a faraway exit, one that joins up with all the other legs we've discovered over the years? Maybe it even shakes hands with Aladdin II?

Jett taps his watch, and I nod. "Ten minutes max, I get it."

Less than five minutes later, we come to a narrowing with stalactites and stalagmites that meet so solidly it's like jaws on a snarling T-Rex with the top and bottom teeth touching. The fangs span the little tunnel from left to right, so tightly grouped that there seems no way through without a dental sledgehammer.

"Whoa, this is so unusual," I say. "Dad would be into the geology of this."

Jett scratches his head. "We're not getting through them without breaking them, which is definitely against caving code."

"But someone has already broken one," I say, rubbing a gloved finger on a stubby stalagmite to the far right that no longer touches its ceiling-anchored partner. Focusing my light on the formation, I scratch my head. "Not a natural break. Sawn off."

"Your point is?"

"Someone has been through here before. Someone very skinny. Mica?"

It goes so quiet in T-Rex Cavern that I can hear my own heartbeat, maybe Jett's too. Shadows seem to flicker on the wall, and the air we're following feels like the cave breathing, in and out. Hair rises on the back of my neck. With the utmost care, since I don't want to damage the formations—or my privates—I squeeze through the micro-gap above the broken tooth, er, fang. It requires the determination and flexibility of a limbo dancer. Again, not a chance Dad could fit without some destruction.

"Oh no you don't!" Jett objects, hands on the fangs. "If I can't go, you can't go. Get back here. We're done for today! We shouldn't have come in here in the first place. We need to get out of here, now!"

"Two minutes, Jett. That's all I'm asking," I say from the other side of the fangs. I hand him my cellphone and take two dozen steps forward before hearing a small splash at my feet. Directing my light downward, I see I'm ankle-deep in a sump, a tunnel flooded to the brim. I keep walking until the water is up to my neck and I'm a stone's throw from a towering wall. It's part solid slab and part rocks crammed so tightly together that even a salamander would turn back. It's an uncompromising cul-de-sac and it's very cold.

Raising my light to the ceiling almost two storeys above, I see where the air is still snaking in. There's a tiny slot like an attic window, unreachable without scaffolding. I dare not attempt to climb the wall as the loose rocks in it would likely avalanche down on me at the slightest touch.

I retreat to water's edge to study my map and swallow a lump in my throat. "The Castle! It's the Castle, Jett!" I shout excitedly, unsure whether he can hear me. "There's no way through right here, but the Castle is the other side of this wall!"

We just need to find the Door.

CHAPTER SEVENTEEN

I'm not sure how Jett responds, because I'm already diving head-first into the sump to see if there's an underwater way through. Swimming to the base of the wall, I move my hands along its slimy bottom and surface, searching for a hole, a chink, anything that would permit a skinny, determined caver through to the other side, or offer hope of expanding a peek-hole if we were to return with tools.

My fingers hit a groove, and I follow it like a scientist might feel the outlines of a caveman's drawings. The crease is like a hairline fracture that runs diagonally up, then straight across, then diagonally down, as if this is where an architect has marked out his intention to insert a large fireplace. Disappointed, I surface for air, again ignoring Jett's loud pleading, and dive back down to investigate further. I run my hands all along the underwater barrier, searching for more veins in the rock, or better yet, a hole. My fingers begin to follow another rut, one that forms a circle. Too strange! Then I feel a chipped-out rectangle outline. A trapezoid, a circle, a rectangle. Huh? I feel the lines like a blind person reading Braille script.

The next time I surface to pull oxygen into my lungs, I shout, "Just one more minute, Jett."

His voice, more urgent now, fades as I sink back down to the bottom, feet-first and facing the wall, the barrier I'd give anything to break through.

My hand brushes something that isn't rock. An iron arch embedded in the wall, like an eyebrow high above that fireplace marking. Could it be a door?

I lower myself just a bit farther, only to smash my junk on a protrusion. Arghh! Even when I head up for air, I'm almost too doubled over with pain to breathe.

"What?" comes Jett's panicked voice. Okay, I know I'm breaking all the rules and upsetting Jett, but I can't stop myself. As soon as I can, I sink back into the depths, holding myself far enough away from the wall now that I can identify the castration rock before it attacks me again.

I find it, all right. A foot or two below the iron arch. It's round, large, and feels like rusted iron. It can only be a doorknob. All these years we've been joking about the actual Door connecting the two cave systems, and here, right in front of my eyes, right in my hands…

Too excited to bother surfacing for an oxygen top-up, I yank on the knob, try turning it, and it does turn a little. Then I try moving it up, down, and sideways, digging small rocks out from around it. Curiously, I determine that I can't pull it out toward me because it's attached to a rod. But as I claw gravel out from above and beneath it, it begins to drop.

Just as my lungs are close to exploding, my knees touch something odd—something else that feels like iron, inset into the stone wall like the arch above. An upside-down eyebrow beneath the doorknob.

That's when the rest of the small rocks between the doorknob and the lower iron piece pour out like money from a slot machine. The ball drops from my hands and hits the iron rim beneath, emitting the underwater dong of a church bell—impossibly fast, full, and loud. My head jerks back even as I vaguely recall that sound waves are louder underwater.

Shocked, I grab one of the falling rocks—only to realize it's not a rock but… a bone. Visibility isn't great underwater, but when I bring it close to my face it looks like a human bone. An arm bone or something. I wave it through the water like a madman until I manage to unclench my hand and drop it. It sinks slowly to the bottom of the sump, disappearing into the muck I've raised with my flailing feet.

Sunken church. Drowned congregation. Haunted churchyard. Oh my God, I've dropped the bell clapper on the sideways-lodged bell. The bell of the original church tower. The bell that sank along with my grandfather and the rest of the congregation, too far for anyone to ever find.

Body tremors overtake me. I begin to claw at my own cheeks. For the second time in as many minutes, I have to stop myself from screaming, given that I could drown by taking in water.

I burst out of the water to hear Jett shouting as he attempts to twist his bulk through the too-narrow gap in the fangs. Shrieking now, I fling myself toward the dino jaws, push Jett back, and squeeze between the jagged teeth, the sharp incisors ripping my back and stomach.

Blood drips from my soaking wet shirt as I duck Jett's arms and scrabble like a crazed lizard for the faraway manhole cover that, I decide now, should have been cemented closed forever.

Imagined white gauzy forms awakened by the church bell press in on me from all sides and howl in my ears. I'm shivering uncontrollably as moist coldness presses against my skin, moans fill my ears, and a desperate urge to look behind me overwhelms me. I've awakened the sleeping dead. The people who sank inside the church are angry with me. I deserve it.

Dad knew. That's why he dismissed the map's shadow.

I've reached the den in the wormhole, my arms wrapped

around my trembling body so the phantoms can't clutch me. That's when Jett tackles me from behind, Ana from in front. Ana? What's she doing here? She doesn't cave anymore.

"Hudson, Hudson, Hudson," they're saying, as the white forms scatter and the squealing in my ears slowly fades. Jett has tackled me to the floor and pinned my shoulders while Ana stands there with her hands cupping my face. Jett removes his sweatshirt to press it against my bleeding back.

"Stop screaming! What happened, Huds? Are you okay?" Jett's voice.

I try to speak, but only a gurgle escapes. *Dad knew.*

"Get him to the top," Jett says tersely.

Somehow, the two of them manage to haul me along and march, push, and coax me to and up the rungs. Jett, who appears to have acquired super-human strength, lifts the heavy iron lid like it's a beret. He has barely scrambled into the street when I tumble on top of him, and Ana on me. Trog leaps about licking all our faces. Raindrops splatter the dusty street, raising a strong, earthy smell. The downpour erases much of the blood on my clothing.

A car horn honks, but the driver veers around us. My pulse is racing, but I'm starting to come back to myself. Erin is speeding by on her bicycle when she spots us. Better her than the police, right? Better her than my dad, for sure.

"Hey, guys, you okay? What're you up to?"

"Just repositioning this manhole cover so it doesn't clank so much when car tires run over it," I hear myself say. She can't know. No one should know. If my dad finds out that I disrespected the dead...

"Can I help?" She steps off her bike, her hand shielding her eyes from the rain.

"Nah, we've got it," Ana says, a little too sharply.

Erin shrugs, gets back on her bike, and rides away.

As Ana struggles to drag the manhole cover back on, Jett and I join in the effort, elbowing the prancing dog aside. I feel Dad's disapproval and anger, anguish and agony, pressing down like a weight on my neck.

"Hudson? You look like you've seen a ghost," Ana is saying. I crave a hug from her, but she looks half frightened of me. "What happened? I take it mission was not accomplished?"

I shake my head, half hoping, expecting to hear the firehall bell ringing. Anything to convince me that the deafening bell reverberation underwater was not my doing, that maybe there was no underwater bell at all. I feel like I'm stuck in a nightmare. But there's no emergency bell clanging. No fire engines or police cars or people running for shelter. No newly sunken craters, shaking ground, crackling fire, or flooding river. No tsunami racing toward us from the bay. And no one paying any attention to three soaking wet teens and an oversize dog sitting on the curb a short distance from Tass Gas, one of them—me—looking like he's been hit by a stun gun.

"Huds?" Jett says gently, taking my cellphone from his pocket, studying it, then handing it back. "Your mom's called five times in the past half hour."

My foggy brain fires up. *Five times? That's not like Mom. What's happened?*

I listen to her last voice message and look up, stricken. "There's been an accident. Dad's in the hospital. I gotta go."

CHAPTER EIGHTEEN

The hospital walls are green. My mother's face is white. I'm holding her clammy, trembling hand in the waiting area as we wait to hear about Dad, victim of a workplace accident.

When I asked Mom for information, she started sobbing.

"Critical condition. Head injury," the nurses tell us. "The doctor will be with you soon."

What does "soon" mean?

I picture the day that TT's machinery depot parking lot collapsed while Jett and I were almost directly underneath it, admiring Pool Dome. I recall emerging to find bosses in safety vests lined up on an unsafe tongue of dirt, fretting over the damage. A red backhoe teetering on the edge of the collapsed surface. A giant dump-truck up to its windshield in muddy water four storeys below.

Me talking to Mr. Toop: "*Lucky you didn't lose more than one rig. But this sinkhole here is still seriously unstable.*"

And Mr. Toop's reply: "*I'm sure my safety officers can take care of things from here, Gear or whoever you are.*"

I understand now. No safety officers climbed in those vehicles that week, nor did they rig up cables to pull them back from the brink. Instead, they probably argued among themselves as to what was the safest measure, until they agreed to put Dad in charge. Why endanger more junior employees when he alone had the guts, experience, and willingness to get those vehicles back to safe ground? Today was the day. Dad's passing comment at breakfast—*Gotta retrieve some engines today before they belly-flop*—hadn't even registered with me. He's an old hand at driving every sort of TT vehicle. He wouldn't put himself in danger. Safety cables would be involved.

I hang my head. Safety matters. All safety. I think about all the stupid chances I've taken, like with the Rule of Three, because I thought I was too good or too smart. Something could have gone wrong, like it almost did with Mica that day, and with me today in that underwater tomb.

Tass is full of hidden caves waiting to snatch whatever is above them, like carnivorous plants that trap and roll up prey in their innocent-looking leaves. The hollows lurk like they're entitled to break out and bask in daylight whenever they feel the urge. It's like they want to take over the world, swallowing one piece of Tass at a time. I picture one patch of earth swallowing the church all those decades ago. Digesting an entire congregation, including Mica's and my forebears, without so much as a burp. The citizens' bones lie deep underground, underwater, undiscovered, untouched. Until today.

I sit up straight when a white-coated guy with a stethoscope around his neck heads our way. I don't recognize him. He must be new to Tass. He looks weary and sad. I tense.

"Mrs. Greer? And—?"

"Hudson, our son," she says. I rise before Mom does and shake the doctor's hand.

"I'm Dr. Garcia." He waves us into a small, stuffy room with a clipboard in his hand.

"Your husband, your father, has a severe concussion and body bruises from the machine's fall. I understand the edge of the sinkhole widened as he started up the vehicle. The steel safety cable snapped, and the tractor toppled over and landed upside down on a new shoulder of the pit. He's extremely lucky it didn't roll all the way down in. He's very fortunate to be alive."

We wait. My stomach is pure acid. My nerves are zinging. Mom is statue-still, studying the beige linoleum floor.

"It's what we call a closed head injury, when the head snaps back and forward without actual skull damage. This can cause traumatic brain injury," Dr. Garcia continues. "He will hopefully make a full recovery, but we'll keep him for observation for a day or two to monitor any increased cranial pressure, swelling, or a bleed. When he returns home, keep him in a quiet room with soft light. He may experience problems with speech and balance, migraines, drowsiness, and difficulty thinking. It's important he rests so the brain can heal."

The doctor's voice is even, gentle, and all too practised. But that doesn't ease my seized-up guts as my mind plays an endless visual loop of Dad's tractor somersaulting with him into the widening mouth of that pit.

No one could have predicted if or when the edges of the newly formed crater would collapse and widen the hole. How was anyone to know there was such a thin layer of rock between parking lot and cave ceiling in the first place? There are instruments that can measure such things if technicians are simultaneously beneath and on top of the ceiling, of course, but no way did Ms. Mast ever organize a professional crew to take one of those devices—a transponder—into caves around here. One thing I'm sure of: The pit would neither have formed nor widened if TT had tighter policies and safety precautions.

"Greedy-guts, ignoring science and clear warning signs in order to milk more money from the land," Mr. Williams mumbled once during work on our science project. *"They think they can get away with it."*

Mom stands and smooths her skirt. "Thank you, doctor. Can we see him now?"

"Very briefly, but you need to understand he is not responsive at this point."

When I enter his room, I feel like I'm in a cave, one that smells of urine and disinfectant. A computer screen near the head of the bed is beeping. Dad's lying on his back, stiff white sheets pulled up to his chin, his mountain of a chest rising and lowering rhythmically. Bruises peek out from the edges of his blue hospital gown: pools of angry black and blue that extend up his neck, chin, and face.

Mom laces her fingers through Dad's and presses her lips to his forehead. "You'll be home soon, dear," she tells him, a tear splashing onto his cheek. "We're right here."

I place a hand on his shoulder: a feather-light, almost fearful touch.

Dad, we found the Castle-Dungeon connection, but you'd have been really upset to see it, and I'm never going to be able to tell you about it. I'm sorry. I don't really say that. I am struggling too hard not to cry. I brush a finger across his forehead, above the closed eyes.

"It's dark in here so you can recover," I whisper. "Dark like a healing cave, okay? We'll be with you every day until you're ready to come home." My voice cracks when I say, "We love you."

I want his eyelids to flutter open, his strong arm to pat me on the back, a grin to break out on his face. *Took a tractor for a carnival ride today, son. Craziest stunt I've ever done. No worries. I'll be back up and at it in no time, ready for Aladdin II or anywhere else you want to explore. It's all good. Just a few weeks of rest needed.*

A nurse enters to usher us out.

We return to the waiting room where we hunker down in worn chairs, neither of us mentioning supper or home. Every molecule of me is saturated with tiredness, denial, and frustration. My mind wants to shut down. I stare at a smudge on the floor as carts of linens, supplies, and dinner trays pass by.

A pair of black, well-polished men's dress shoes comes into view and pauses. A pair of very high red heels follows and halts at the edge of my vision. Mom shifts like she's going to rise, but doesn't. I look up and involuntarily shrink back. It's Mr. Toop with his executive secretary, Trina.

"I'm so sorry, Mrs. Greer," says Toop.

"So am I, Lucy and Hudson," adds Trina.

Trina moves directly to Mom, where the woman blinks her false eyelashes and bends down to embrace my mother's small frame.

"Thank you," Mom mumbles. "They say he's likely to make a full recovery, but it will… take time."

I look at Trina, then press my back into the upholstered chair to scan Mr. Toop's face. He's faking sympathy. He's holding something behind his back.

"It was a very unfortunate mishap," Mr. Toop says. "A freak accident. I'm so glad to hear he'll be okay. In the meantime, the company would naturally like to offer you as much time off as you need, Mrs. Greer, and get supplemental health-cost benefits flowing to you immediately. Toward that end, Mrs. Phelps and I have brought a document to speed up the process. Are you up to signing it, Mrs. Greer?"

A paper comes out from behind his back, and a pen somehow transfers to Mom's right hand. Trina holds onto her left hand as if Mom will need that grip in order to do the right thing.

Mom raises the pen and presses the paper to the side table beside her—

"No, Mom!" I say, and our visitors jump slightly. "You don't sign something you haven't read. And this is hardly the time or place for anyone to be pressuring you into putting a signature on a contract."

"Hudson, you're speaking out of turn," Mom warns, but in a weak, wavering voice.

"Son," Mr. Toop says, addressing me fake-gently, "I know it's a difficult moment for your family, but that is exactly why this is the right time. We want to take financial stress off your mother so she can tend to your father as needed."

How dare he talk about Mom like that when she's right next to us! Okay, so he's both my mom's and dad's boss. I have no right at all. But I'm going to ignore manners and job security in this moment!

"Leave. Us. Alone." With teeth gritted, I snatch the paper from Mom and place it behind my back. My face feels tight, my body rigid. There's a pain in the back of my throat and roaring in my ears as I ignore Mom's raised eyebrow or the stares from staff at the nurses' station. "Dad could have died. He's hurt because—because—"

I can't squeeze out the words "of you." But we lock eyes—his seem to turn cold—and Trina drops Mom's hand.

"You're right, dear," Mom says tiredly, like she has been roused from sleep. "We'll take it and look it over, Trina. Thank you, Mr. Toop." She's tugging on a strand of hair and rocking back and forth. In her spaced-out state, Mom may not recall that a week ago this man didn't know her name.

Mr. Toop's nostrils flare as he busies himself straightening his tie. Trina pastes on a smile. Their postures admit defeat.

"We'll leave it with you, then, and be in touch," Trina says, patting my mother's hand with her own manicured one. Mr. Toop and Trina leave quickly and silently down the hall. Mom watches them vaguely.

Me, I'm tempted to spit in their direction. That contract is surely nothing but bad news for us, preventing any chance of suing or some such. *Do I actually want to date the daughter of someone like this?*

Dad's accident, the parking-lot collapse, the danger to the community centre, the sham of an inspector…

I turn to take both my mother's hands and raise them gently to my face, lost for words.

CHAPTER NINETEEN

"Dude, you going to the protest or not?" Jett's on the phone, referring to the crowds gathering on TT headquarters' well-clipped lawn.

Ever since the parking-lot sinkhole, there have been grumblings from townspeople about TT's practices. The complaints have multiplied since Dad got hurt, stoked by Mr. Williams, who is rumoured to have recently experienced a suspicious flat tire, an emptied gas-tank incident, and nasty words spray-painted on his front door.

"Jett, both my mom and dad work there." Yes, I totally blame TT for Dad's accident now, whether there's proof that sinkhole formed and then expanded due to sloppy policy enforcement or not. My rage against the company brews like an ulcer. Maybe my recent fright underground intensifies it. I've been picking fights with kids on the school basketball court for no reason, sometimes even being rude to Mom. I've slammed my fist into the wall outside our house more than a few times. Even now, there's a pounding in my ears. But that thin thread of reason, my mother's cautions, and my responsibilities at home, have kept me from doing anything rash.

"You wouldn't be the only TT-connected protester. Why do you think your dad got hurt? We want better safety rules. Grow a pair, Huds."

I press my lips together. I respect my caving partner, but I just don't think this protest is the best use of our time. Indeed, just hearing his voice reminds me that we've done very little caving in the past few days, and I need to go underground to work out all my frustration.

A moan comes from down the hall.

"Jett, Dad needs me. I'll text if I can make it." There's a sigh on the other end of the line as I kill the call and hurry to Dad's bedroom. He hasn't spoken more than an occasional one-syllable word since he was released from the hospital. He just lies in bed waiting for us to deliver food or a bedpan. His visiting speech therapist says to be patient. His bruises have gone through a kaleidoscope of colour changes and are now mostly faded, but he still prefers a dark cloth over his eyes, shades down, and lights out. His migraines must be fierce but will ease up eventually, the doctor promised us.

Mom and I take turns perching on his patchwork quilt to keep him company. He moans loudly if anyone's not in the room when he needs something, so one of us is always within earshot.

Today I move his water glass and its drinking straw to his dry lips, and am rewarded by an "Mmm," which I've learned means "Thank you."

He pats the bedspread, and I plunk down there ready to recount caving adventures we've enjoyed together, which he seems to like. He squeezes my hand.

"There's a protest up at TT at the moment," I tell him. "People wanting more transparency on the company's operations, more promises of safety. Because of the parking-lot sinkhole and your accident."

He says nothing, doesn't move.

"Jett wants me to go, but I don't want to get you and Mom in trouble."

"G-g-go."

He actually said "go?" Wait....

"You want me to go?"

His chin dips in a half nod.

We sit quietly for a while, me unsure how to answer and wondering if he has fallen asleep again. Then he squeezes my hand. "C-c-caving?" A smile forms beneath his mask.

I draw a deep breath. "Jett, Ana, and I found a new passage, Dad."

He holds up three fingers, then an upraised thumb, as if to approve that I am caving with a full contingent, and he grips my hand tightly. He appears to be keen for me to continue. I'd love to add that Ana seems into me, but it's not like I've had time to follow through on the movie date.

"We went down the manhole cover behind Tass Gas."

His entire body stiffens, his chest rising and falling fitfully.

"It led to a tunnel that ended in a sump and a wall, but I think we were close to the Dungeon-Castle join, Dad."

Dad's right hand lifts toward his bedside table, gently touching his beloved church model, which Mom has moved here from the desk in the den. His pill bottles sit next to it.

"You need more painkiller?" I ask.

"N-n-no." He squeezes his eyes shut, opens them again. Then he drops his hands back on the bed and turns away from me. Am I imagining it, or does a tear slip out from under an eye? "T-t-tired."

"Okay, Dad, but you're improving, you know." Should I not have mentioned the new passage? I back out slowly.

"Mom?" I ask as she appears at the top of the stairs.

"Yes, Hudson."

"Going for a bike ride if that's okay."

"Good, dear. Get some exercise and fresh air. I'm here."

She forgets to warn me away from the protest. Or maybe she doesn't know or care it's happening.

CHAPTER TWENTY

I'm halfway to the crowd I can see gathering up on the hill when thirst urges me to stop at Jukebox, a tiny café that sells cold drinks. Its back screen door slams as I park my bike nearby and there's Erin, frowning and hauling a bag of trash to the rusty Dumpster.

"Hey, Hudson." She brightens. "I've just finished my shift. Are you heading to the protest?"

"Um, yeah, after I get a lemonade."

"Okay. It's on me. Back in a sec." She opens the door wide and wedges a rock against it to hold it that way while I wait. I peer in while she joins a co-worker behind the counter—and freeze. Only two customers are inside: Mica and Ana. They're sharing the same booth, leaning in, and giggling way too cozily. I back up before they can see me, a burning sensation in my chest, flashes at the edge of my vision.

Erin reappears and presses a cool glass of lemonade into my hands, eyes probing mine.

"They're in here a lot lately, those two."

She must be reading my body language without benefit of her crystal ball. I feel my face flinch like someone has slapped it.

"Come on," she says, "let's see what's happening up the hill. Got a bandana in case there's tear gas?"

She's joking, I tell myself.

"So, that manhole cover you guys were messing with last week led to a cave," Erin says unexpectedly, studying my face as we slow on a steep rise.

"And you think that for what reason?" I reply, trying to keep my tone neutral and hide any surprise or annoyance.

She shrugs. "Just not sure why you felt you had to lie to me. I'm not an idiot, you know. It doesn't take three people to rearrange a manhole cover, one of them soaking wet and shook-up looking. If it was some big new find, it's not like I'd broadcast it to your rival cave gang."

"Like Ana has?" I press.

"I didn't say that." She crosses her arms and walks a little faster.

Big new find. That's definitely what the T-Rex sump wall was beneath the manhole. And sometime, somehow, someone had been there before, chipping a tooth to wriggle through. Jett and I couldn't figure it out. Could it have been Mica?

I pick up my pace. I want to ask more, or try again in a different way, but a stubbornness against playing whatever her game is kicks in. So I change the subject.

"Guess we can't expect those two to show their faces at the protest," I venture.

"Guess not." She sounds almost smug. "Their daddies might take a belt to their hides. Speaking of which, occasionally Ana comes in with her dad. Sometimes I hear what they're saying."

"Yeah?"

"The other day I heard Mr. Toop say, 'The sooner we find it, the sooner we can get out of this hick town.' And Ana said, 'Not fast enough for me. This place sucks.'"

It, it, what is *it*? And why do they want to leave town when they find *it*? I can make no sense out of that. "She's just saying whatever will make her dad happy, and we don't know what the context was." I don't add that I'm more worried Ana has tipped Mica off about T-Rex Cavern, if he didn't know about it already. And I'm pretty steamed that Ana might see something in Mica.

But also confused, given that someone seemed to have found that T-Rex sump wall before Jett and me, which means maybe Mica didn't need Ana's inside info.

Anyway, what happened to the Ana-and-me vibe? Does she move on that fast, or is two-timing her thing? Just because I've been busy with my dad shouldn't mean—

"No more disasters... Safety matters... We want answers!" a crowd is chanting up ahead.

"Doesn't quite rhyme," I observe. "Wonder who came up with that."

"Yeah, well, Mr. Williams is a science teacher, not a poet." Erin points to his figure standing on a giant boulder covered in velvet green moss close to TT headquarters' property line. He looks like a band conductor, hands in the air waving a megaphone, egging on the crowd from his plush podium.

I look around and recognize most of the people, of course, even a brave few who work at TT. There are school friends, including Dirk pumping his fist, shouting, and bouncing on the balls of his feet. That doesn't surprise me, given he's drawn to troublemaking. There's the town bus driver, the guy who runs the marina, fish-plant employees, and a few fishermen, all waving their arms, yelling, getting into it. Also, some of the young drifters who work at a cooperative organic farm up the road.

More strangely, there are a bunch of twenty-something men built like tanks that I've never seen before in my life. A boxer fieldtrip that lost its way? They're mostly wearing black sweatshirts with hoods pulled up, and they're leaping about like pre-show wrestlers warming up, the most raucous of the fifty-some people gathered. A few townspeople, like me, are glancing at them sideways.

"No more sinkholes!" a hand-written placard reads. The person holding it shakes it menacingly in the salt-tinged air.

"Greedy goals lead to sinkholes," another announces.

"A lot of excitement for our sleepy town," I say to Erin.

"Yeah, it's like someone just woke up a colony of wasps." Erin cups her hands around her mouth. "No more disasters! Safety matters!"

Mr. Williams is blowing a whistle and waving at people to calm down. No one has emerged from TT headquarters behind him to meet the protestors. I picture Mr. Toop leading the troops down secret stairs to a bunker that will become the town's next sinkhole.

This is my parents' workplace and some of these are their workmates. Honest people with honest jobs for a corporation that may or may not be honest. TT just needs a team of genuine inspectors and a safety-regulations overhaul. It doesn't take a scientist to know that building roads and uprooting trees beside streams in sinkhole terrain is a dumb idea. Dad has been seriously injured, and the community centre is threatening to sink. Maybe it's okay to feel bitter.

"Clear-cut logging has accelerated fourfold here in the past year, causing instability in our building foundations," Mr. Williams shouts. "You've all seen more cracks form in your houses, right?"

"Right!" comes a loud chorus.

"Landslides downslope of new logging roads have caused cloudiness in our drinking water. One token inspector—I repeat, *token* inspector—has approved everything TT is up to, while we, the hardworking citizens of Tass, get no full-disclosure and no say at all."

"Yeah! TT cares about profits, not people!" a heckler shouts.

"The recent sinkhole was no random act of nature," Mr. Williams continues, speaking without notes. "Nor was that sinkhole's sudden widening, which nearly killed a TT worker recently."

"Shut 'em down!" someone shouts. "Bring in the Feds!"

"Company don't tell us nothin'!" someone adds. "Gonna kill us cuttin' all them trees down and buildin' roads where roads ain't meant to be!"

"No more disasters! Safety matters!" Was that me cupping my hands around my mouth and cheering on my ex-teacher?

Erin smiles at me like she's proud. Little does she know about the thin scab over a boil inside my chest right now. I want to run up to headquarters and break a window. Shake someone or something down. My whole body is trembling as Mr. Williams continues to work the crowd with facts, science, and rhetorical questions.

"Why do they target only the oldest, biggest, and most solid trees for chopping down?" he asks. "Why do they clear-cut deep in the forest and build roads without going through proper community protocols? I'll tell you why."

"Greedy bastards!" someone with a long beard and sitting in a wheelchair in the crowd replies. "I remember when our water was clear! We were here before TT. We'll be here after they scram, leavin' us nothin'. Run 'em outta town!"

The crowd claps wildly, some people dancing in place. That's when a grey sedan cruises down the gravel road above headquarters. It brakes so fast it's like the driver wants the dust cloud to choke people gathered.

Out steps Mr. Toop, his ever-present heavies, and Mayor Brown, in suits and ties that they dust off for effect.

"Mr. Toop's ride needs a carwash," Erin says, elbowing me, and I can't help grinning.

Mr. Toop saunters over to speak to Mr. Williams, who leans down and hands the big boss his bullhorn.

"We thank you for your concern and recognize your right to gather," Mr. Toop begins, his voice as smooth as the waves washing the shore below. "And we aim to answer your questions right here, today, if we can. But we'd also like to emphasize that sinkholes have plagued this region for decades, centuries even, and—" He gets no further before a rock sails through the air and ricochets off his shoulder.

"Don't give us no more bull!" a male voice shouts.

"Uh-oh," Erin mumbles.

I scan the crowd to search for his assailant and see people cheering on one of the hoodies from out of town.

"Folks, folks! Calm down," Mayor Brown intones, though he looks a little shaken. "Let's listen to one another respectfully. TT clears trees that pose fire risks to Tass, and for any operations, they submit their plans to City Council after an inspector—"

"Mayor's in TT's pocket!" someone shouts. "How much they pay you, Brown-Noser?"

A wine bottle sails through the air, narrowly missing Mayor Brown, and smashes on Mr. Williams's boulder. I see people bending down to pick up other objects, presumably to toss. Despite my own grudges against TT, I'm shocked when Dirk scoops up a sharp-looking piece of rubble and sends it flying over Mr. Toop's head.

Mr. Williams grabs back the megaphone. "Let the men speak!" he says, just as a tomato splats in his face. There's laughter, then angry people shouting as the crowd surges forward. As

Mr. Williams scrambles off his boulder and starts running up the gravel road toward his house, punks close the gap between themselves and the men on the hill, objects flying.

Police sirens sound as six squad cars speed down the road in the direction that Mr. Toop's sedan had come from moments earlier. Where did they come from? Tass has one squad car on a good day. Someone must have called in reinforcements from who-knows-where—reinforcements that were hiding around the corner on the assumption this would go bad.

I grab Erin and pull her back. "We need to get out of here."

"Rental hooligans," she says, initially resisting my tug, then dodging a flying clump of dirt and wisely deciding to follow me downhill toward the Jukebox.

"What do you mean?" I ask.

"TT buses in thugs to make the event turn violent so they can arrest the lot of us and tamp down protest," she says. "See the two guys filming the whole thing from the roof of TT? Recording our faces so the company knows who to fire if rental cops don't get them in the next few minutes."

I look back to see police push Dirk roughly to the ground, press his face into the gravel, and handcuff him along with a few others at the front. Seriously? I feel like I'm watching a bad movie. "How do you know all this? Or what makes you think you know?"

Erin winks. "A history paper I wrote on Russian coup methods. That I got an A on."

I have no idea if she's deadpanning or not. Nor do I get a chance to figure it out, 'cause just then I see Mom running out of our house, gesturing wildly for me to come home. Seconds later, a big stick soars through the air and slams into her shoulder, nearly knocking her off her feet. She leans down, picks it up, and examines it with a stunned expression. One of the cops who's definitely not from Tass sprints to her, whirls her around, and orders her to lie on the ground.

"What?" she asks helplessly as Erin and I rush to her aid.

"I'm arresting you for helping to incite a riot," the officer barks. "You need to come to the station for questioning." He points to two vanloads already stuffed to capacity with Tass citizens looking confused and aghast.

Mom's dull blue eyes rise to mine. Her voice when she speaks is tight. "Go home and look after your father."

CHAPTER TWENTY-ONE

Everything is my fault, I reflect miserably as I lie beside my softly snoring father on my parents' queen-size bed. First, I let Mr. Williams talk me into giving a presentation at the community centre. It probably put my entire family on someone's radar as troublemakers.

Then I risked getting Mom in trouble when I photographed TT maps on the sly. Maps that influenced Dad, Jett, and me to go exploring under TT land—in the Aladdin Cave—and discover a new, under-wraps worksite that offered proof of TT's unsafe work practices.

Worse, I was there when Dad said he was going to pull vehicles out of the danger zone that morning. Why didn't I pay more attention? I should have insisted he wait until we did our own inspection of the site. He might not have listened, but at least I could have tried. Mom and I should have begged him not to go.

At the hospital, I was rude to Mr. Toop, a dumb move even if he was trying to pull a fast one with that contract, which Mom never did sign.

Finally, I attended a protest today that was rigged, a trap, and Mom's belated worry about me being there got her arrested. Will she get fined? Possibly fired? How will our family eat and live?

I press my hands on my eyes to block out the world. Here I am running around as if discovering a join between two cave systems is more important than my family or town. Driven in part by my petty rift with Mica, my pursuit of fame and fortune has made me ignore safety more than once. Mr. Williams was right all along. TT's projects are wreaking havoc with Tass's already fragile infrastructure, and another major sinkhole is just waiting to happen.

Dad and I have the instruments and know-how to attempt an early warning on when or where it could occur. Well, there's Mica and Ana too, but they're on the wrong side of all this. And not to be trusted, I remind myself, as I revisit the image of the two of them leaning their heads together in that booth, and then Erin adding that Ana and Mica have been hanging together.

Mica, who was using his connections to get what he could from Ms. Mast. Mica, who makes my life miserable because I suffered a months-ago fall that happened to plug up "his" cave entrance at the wrong moment. Rotten luck. Or were we already drifting apart as he got more hypercompetitive about finding the Door and meaner to everyone as his parents spent less and less time with him? And then there's the Ana factor. We're competing for the attention of someone who doesn't seem all that interested in either of us, if I'm honest. Which doesn't do much for Mica's and my relationship, either.

And yet, competing with Mica to find the potential portal is now just an embarrassing memory. Becoming celebrated cave explorers who would bring the world to Tass's new commercial mega-cave was a selfish, childish dream. I have a new goal: to get to a cave beneath the community centre to assess its danger to the town. I recall seeing a curious dip out the back door of the centre. Maybe it could lead to a new cave entrance?

Unfortunately, the manhole route was a dead end—a crazy, spooky one at that—so I need to come in from the other side.

That involves a whole new study of the maps that Dad keeps in his safe in the den next door. There are maps on the wall, but those are totally generic. The only two maps outside the safe—sitting on top of it, in fact—are the stolen TT map and the one Dad and I were creating by merging its information and ours. Come to think about it, Dad has never taken all the maps out at the same time. It's possible there are some I've never seen that might reveal something crucial. Like where I could find an undiscovered entrance to that centre-of-town subterranean space.

I don't know the code for the safe's combination lock. Maybe Mom does. Or maybe Dad can try to tell me when he wakes up. Turning my head, I get all choked up at the sight of the helpless figure beside me. In that darkened room, for the first time since his accident, I allow tears to slip down my face.

Without stirring from my position, I try phoning Mom, but there's no reply. A lump forms in my throat and my palms begin to sweat. When will she get home? They'll surely let her free after they realize it's all a terrible mix-up. The videographers on TT's roof will have footage that clears her, right? I can't have an injured father and jailed mother. What would I do?

As dusk takes away what little light was leaking through the room's windows, tiredness washes over me. I glance again at my peacefully sleeping, slowly healing father, and at the little church model on his side table. I struggle to stay awake....

Sometime later my eyelids jerk open. Groggy from an unexpectedly deep sleep, I turn to note that Dad remains sleeping beside me. I check the clock and see I've slept for a couple of hours. The house is deadly quiet, so what could have woken me? I'm certain something did. As Dad and I lie there in his murky room, I have a strong sense of someone being in the house, someone creeping about. Maybe Mom is home?

There's a soft crinkle of paper and a barely audible click—from the den next door, I judge. Then a footfall. Just one. My senses go on hyper alert. I resist calling out for Mom. She would not be sneaking around in the den. Rising super slowly, I look around for something with which to protect myself—and Dad. Just off their bedroom is Mom's sewing nook. I lift a small pair of scissors from a basket beside her sewing machine.

Sounds again. *Shuffle, shuffle, click.* The clicks sound like Dad's safe's lock being turned. Does this intruder know the combination? Tass doesn't get break-ins like cities do. They're almost unheard of in our town.

My bare feet glide along the carpet, out Mom and Dad's bedroom door, and into the hallway. I lean a nose-length past the den's door frame, enough to observe. There's a flashlight moving in there. It's trained on the safe, where a tall man's fingers are twisting the lock this way and that. He's dressed totally in black, including a hoodie. I hold my breath. My heart is trying to thump its way out of my chest.

I think of retreating and calling 911, but no one would get here in time. Nor do I even trust the police anymore. Like the mayor, they may be in TT's pocket. Slowly, I slip my phone out of my pocket. A surprise photo might identify the housebreaker before he dashes away. But first I count to ten, waiting to see if he actually opens the safe. Nope. I hear a soft grunt as he starts trying a new series of numbers.

My sweaty palm grips the sewing scissors.

Throat tight, I aim my phone and press the button. *Click.* The dark figure spins around, lunges, and tackles me head-to-chest while trying to grab the phone, but my foot is out and he trips, falls, and tumbles headfirst down the stairs.

I race down and leap on him.

"Mica?" My muscles go rigid and my head jerks back. "What the—?"

"It's not what you think, Hudson," he says, crumpled on the lower landing, hair covering his eyes.

"Oh yeah? And what would I think, Mica? That you're trying to break into my dad's safe?"

His shoulders slump. He rolls onto his back and clasps his hands in his lap. "Your dad has maps—"

"We have maps, yes," I say slowly, harshly.

"—that you and I both need. To save the town."

"Ha! Now you're a saviour, are you? Just 'cause you've been caught? Everyone knows what you really are, Mica. But even I didn't think you'd stoop this low."

He takes a ragged breath. "I'm really sorry about your dad, Hudson. And your mom tonight."

"Really?" I cross my arms over my chest. "Or glad, because it made a break-in easier? Are you trying to steal maps to make a name for yourself? Or did your dad send you so TT can get hold of them and destroy them?" I pause for effect. "Or maybe Ana sent you?"

He raises his head far enough that I can see him grit his teeth. Then he goes unnaturally still. Finally, he straightens his shoulders, and his eyes turn dark. "Like you're innocent, having stolen TT maps to merge with yours."

I spot a piece of paper sticking out of his jeans pocket and whip my hand out to grab it. It rips in half as he tries to stop me.

We both go quiet.

"What made you think you could figure out the combination, jerk?"

Mica shrugs. "I know your birthday, your dad's birthdate, your mom's."

"Genius. But those didn't work, did they? Even I don't know the numbers, not that I'd tell you if I did."

"Hudson, I know it looks bad."

"You think?"

"But what Mr. Williams was saying about more and more foundation cracks around town—more of the wilt, tilt, warp... whatever that line is. It's happening. It's speeding up. Dad's worried. I'm worried. You should be worried."

I know the expression. It's for signs of a potential sinkhole: wilt, tilt, warp, crack, and crater. Wilted plants and cloudy water hint that water is being sucked away by an expanding underground hollow. Tilted trees and fenceposts show sinking ground, warped doors and windows indicate the building is shifting, and fractures and craters (shallow new depressions) are obvious warnings.

"Your dad's worried? That'll be the day. He's Mr. Toop's puppet, as far as I can tell. All that money your dad makes for your fancy house and swimming pool and big vacations: How much of it is under-the-table TT payoffs? And now you're in thick with Ana, eh? She's got you breaking into my house to grab maps TT doesn't have? What's next? You'll try to get me in hot water for having one little TT map that happened to be lying on a desk when I was visiting my mom at work?" I wave the torn paper that came from Mica's pocket. "Because it's not enough that both my mom and dad are in deep trouble." Now I'm choking up, which is the last thing I want Mica to see. So I spit out the next bit.

"Let me ask you this one more time, Mica Brown. Who put you up to breaking into our house and trying to steal caving maps we've spent years—Dad has spent decades—making? If not TT or your dad, then it must be all about you trying to get ahead with finding where the cave systems join. No matter which of those is correct, you're a pitiful asswipe. Answer the question!"

He winces. I can't believe I just said that to my former best friend.

"It's none of those," he whines. "I didn't think you'd trust me, or help me, and figured this was the only way. Dad had a falling-out with Mr. Toop tonight, and he has been worried for a while about what Mr. Williams is saying. He lost a grandfather in the Big One, remember, and he and I want to use our caving knowledge—"

"And Dad's and my maps," I say with narrowed eyes.

"—to convince Mr. Toop, or to sway his bigger bosses, or to get the community on the same page. If your dad weren't hurt, maybe he'd help us? And Ana would like to help us convince her father—"

"Oh, now you speak for Ana?"

He doesn't reply. It's better that way.

I bite my lip, blow air into my cheeks, then let it out slowly. I feel like someone has grabbed my feet, whipped me upside down, and shaken me till I don't know which way is up. I'm supposed to suddenly trust Mica, his father, and Ana? Yeah, right!

"*Unnnh!*" comes a sound from upstairs.

Mica looks like he's heard a ghost.

"That's my dad. I need to help him. Get out of here, Mica. Just leave. Don't even think of taking anything with you. And don't ever come back."

He glances once more at the crumpled, torn half-sheet of paper on the stair, empties his pocket of the other form's half, then flees out the door like a blur. He always was fast.

I sit there stunned and confused. Never have I felt so alone or unsure what to do.

I sleep fitfully after Mica leaves, but thankfully Mom is released from the police station early in the morning. That gives me a few hours off from being with Dad this afternoon. Mom probably falsely believes it will help distract me from worrying about how long Dad will be unwell and about how we will cope if Dad never recovers fully. Anyway, that's why I'm huffing up a steep trail to clear my head. I veer off the trail at Ribbon Falls, impulsively deciding to bushwhack up to a stone ridge I haven't visited in a while. Lots of ravens hang out there. It's a great place to take photos, or just remind myself how beautiful this area can be.

I step over a marker that indicates I'm on TT land. Who cares? Along the way, a woodpecker is tapping out long-winded messages, starlings flit out from under my feet, and four deer leap from out of nowhere and crash through the salal.

I've stopped for a snack under an overhang on the ridge. I'm perched like a lifeguard under an umbrella surveying a sea of Douglas fir when the sun catches something glimmering over on the next ridge. Someone with mirrored sunglasses is hiking just the other side. Someone wearing a fashionable hat only a female would wear. Only one female. Could it be Ana?

Curiosity draws me forward. I move down the steep slope slowly, tripping on roots and ignoring the squeak of squirrels. I'm halfway up the other side of the valley but still well under leafy cover when I hear two people speaking: Ana and her father.

I slow, half relieved, half disappointed about her dad's presence. At least they don't know I'm here.

"Can be anywhere from a few feet to a hundred feet thick," Mr. Toop is saying. His voice is as deep as a radio announcer's, but gentle when he's talking with his daughter.

"You want me to crawl in there?" asks Ana, sounding unsurprised but nervous.

I freeze. What would interest a geologist way up here? And why is he encouraging Ana to crawl alone into a hollow? Hasn't he forbidden her from caving around Tass?

"Looks like a granite intrusion," comes a muffled voice a few minutes later: Ana's from underground.

"Good, take photographs a little farther in, and use the axe to pry some rock samples away."

What happened to Rule of Three?

Unintelligible words from Ana.

"Farther in, Ana. We need to be sure."

No, she needs to be safe.

I can no longer hear Ana's voice, but there are a few more muffled exchanges.

"Okay, come on out, honey. That's a contact zone, I'd say. Well done, Ana. Careful, now."

I could finish scrambling up to the ridge, peer over the rim, and ask them what they're up to. I could confront her with what Mica said. A part of me wants to know whether this is some kind of top-secret mission or just a father-daughter geology tutorial. But I end up not moving a muscle till they're gone. They haven't seen or heard me, I can't make sense of anything I've heard, and I've got enough on my mind as it is.

Still, even the short exchange I overheard hasn't made me any fonder of Mr. Toop.

I find myself wondering if Mica was being honest after all when I confronted him last night.

CHAPTER TWENTY-TWO

Lightning skitters across the sky, and a thunderclap all but throws me off my feet.

"Storm's here," I observe, stating the obvious, heart crashing like Ribbon Falls behind me. "This rain is going to turn into torrents in a minute."

Erin adjusts the bright yellow fisherman's hat she's wearing above a too-big matching rain poncho. She looks like a pint-sized fisherman as she stands windblown but determined on top of the keystone of the arched bridge, which amuses me and grows my admiration for her.

"Okay, let's make sure I have this right," she says. "You're not making me go way far into a cave. I just have to sit on this bridge and tip the bottle into the stream in fifteen minutes?" She taps her watch and lifts the 100-millilitre bottle like she's toasting me. "Then I dash to that place called Aladdin's Cave you showed me, poke this ultraviolet flashlight in, and look to see if the dye shows up there."

"Yes, that's right."

"I'm not going to get arrested or poison the town's water supply or drown in the rainstorm or get jumped by TT heavies in the woods on the way back to town? It's just some kind of food colouring?"

"Exactly. It's a non-toxic dye that temporarily turns the water a bright colour. It will flow down the stream into a cave entrance and through the whole cave system till it exits from a resurgence. Jett and I will be waiting at two other resurgences it might show up at."

"And a resurgence is?"

"Where water exits a cave. The fact that this stream is flooding will make the job faster and easier."

"And for this I get a pizza at the one-and-only five-star Tass Gas Pizza, preferably after the rain has stopped?"

"Precisely." I grin at her wry humour. Lucky for me she was up for this. "And you know this is all top secret?"

"Roger that." She salutes. "Not a word to Ana or Mica."

"Okay, fifteen minutes, Erin." I scramble through salal to reach my bike. As heavy rain splats on my face, I put on my helmet and head downhill.

Earlier, I helped Jett down the manhole after making him promise several times that he wouldn't break stalagmites and that he would just go into the sump and peer through the dinosaur teeth to see if it turns fluorescent green. Our flow tracer, as the fluorescent dye is called, can seep through cracks we can't fit through and will travel relentlessly and reliably downstream. If I were a beetle riding on a leaf doing the wild downstream ride from one cave to another, I'd have a finished set of maps by day's end—tinged with gleaming green, of course.

Too bad we don't have dragonfly-size drones to cruise the two cave systems and find all the secret passages between them, Jett had said.

Someday, when we're rich, Jett, I'd replied.

Another bright flash across the sky prompts me to pedal faster. I'm off to the fern-fronted entrance of the cave where I rescued Mica, which I've dubbed Mica's Cave.

Does it fit into the scheme of things? Will its sump turn momentarily green, confirming a connection with the Castle above? Or do Aladdin II, which we haven't explored yet, and that jagged opening I've named T-Rex join up? I wish we had more cave-entrance options and a larger team to watch known exits. I wish we had Dad to help. It has been a couple of days. What if he never gets fully well?

I'm splashing through bike-tire-swallowing puddles as rain pounds my body when I see a streak of white near the community centre. Lightning? A ghost? Be sensible. It looked like a large dog. Trog, the cave-sniffing hound? What's he doing out here in this storm on his own? If I return him to Ana, will she wrap her arms around me in delight? Dream on. He'll find his way home. Anyway, I'm on a mission.

I've turned back toward my intended destination when I hear a pitiful yelp followed by a long, heart-breaking whine. It's so nonstop, I know the dog is in trouble. None of my friends are close enough to have heard him. If I'm super fast at helping the poor thing, I can still get to the dye test in time. I spin around and sprint toward the soaking wet hound, then drop my bike beside him.

He's splayed at the edge of a sunken lawn patch beside the community centre. The patch is full of evil-looking stinging nettles. The wannabe sinkholes in this part of town are fast becoming giant puddles, one of them approaching pond-size. Trog is howling beside the nettles alongside the largest pond. The nettles resemble hairs growing out of a mole.

As I reach the St. Bernard, his pitiful yelps soften. "What's wrong, boy?" My hand follows his leash downward and, ignoring the nettle stings, finds it and one paw, caught. On barbed wire.

"Who is doing this?" I shout into the wind and rain. *Could it be TT?* I run my fingers along the square of vileness until I find one of its anchors. In a rage, my muscles yank it up, peel the barbed wire back, free the paw ever so gently, and lift the dog free. Trog is still in my arms when the ground drops out from under us like quicksand. The freefall is short. I break Trog's fall in a soft mudhole. Silty water pours on top of us as we gasp for breath.

When the ground goes still, I look up like I'm expecting someone to lower a bucket that can haul us back up. As I'm reaching for my cellphone, Trog wriggles so vigorously in my arms that the hole's floor drops another storey, spinning us like a Tilt-a-Whirl connected to a waterslide. Down we go until we're deposited into a cave filled with the echoes of my shouts and Trog's barking.

I'm now covered in muddy slime. Trog resembles a brown bear cub. My entire body goes into shivers, and light-headedness makes it difficult to concentrate. Get it together, Huds. You're a caver.

I feel in my back pockets and pat the rock floor around me. I find my phone and wipe mud off it. Although it won't work underground for phone calls, it provides light. Luckily, too, I'm still wearing my bike helmet. I flick on the phone and train it on the newly formed chute we just slid down. It's slippery with mud, not something anyone could climb back up without help. I move to where Trog is shivering and slowly feel him all over for injuries, muttering reassurances.

As far as I can tell, he's not hurt. I'm not hurt. And we've found a cave under the community centre. At least I have a dog to keep me warm and find me the route out, I reason. But the dye! I moan in disappointment, which attracts a dog tongue on my already wet face.

Standing up, I waver a little, wipe sludge off my face, and wobble a few steps forward. My sneakers splash into water, so

I cast my light all about. It's a grotto the size of an auditorium, with numerous dark cavities around its perimeters that might lead out. But it's a flooded oval. I'm on almost the only dry ground, beside a stream that's hurtling by like it's rush hour. On the other side of the current is one long, shallow mudflat stretching to the far wall.

I aim my light upwards. The ceiling is more than a storey high, with formations filling it like an upside-down garden: rimstone dams and step-like terraces that resemble a fancy fountain in the courtyard of a five-star hotel, and dogtooth spar—a weird name if I ever heard one—pyramid-shaped crystals that look like dog's teeth. This cave even has helictites, a curly version of stalactites that develop from water seeping so slowly through central canals that the calcite crystals form irregular positions at the tips. Like stalactites with a perm.

Customers would pay good money to see this, especially if it's just one stop on a tour from Aladdin to T-Rex. But explaining cave formations to sightseers is not currently a priority.

I picture Erin tipping her bottle in as instructed, jogging down the trail from Ribbon Falls to Aladdin I, and later the manhole, where she'll wait for Jett's head to pop up. Meanwhile, I imagine my caving partner faithfully manning his underground station, peering through fangs of calcite in hopes of spotting a flow of green into what he doesn't know is a haunted sump. Shivers threaten to seize me up for a moment. I'm still half traumatized by the ghosts encountered after I discovered the bell.

But I must concentrate on the present. Will that green flow travel by me enroute to Jett?

If Erin spilled her vial, the sparkling, verdant streak will have left the keystone bridge beside the falls moments ago and coursed through some portion of the two Aladdins, possibly through Mica's Cave, then through spaces that remain blank on our maps—places we've never set foot in.

When the finger of green reaches the far side of the wall in which the church bell and bones are encased, I picture it rising with the swelling current until it pours through the high window like a magical waterfall. Some tracer will squeeze through the hair-wide cracks that seemed to etch a fireplace until the fluorescence illuminates the scary water in which I stood, revealing it as the final barrier holding the Castle and Dungeon apart. Fireplace Wall, I christen it now in my mind. The dazzling display will widen Jett's eyes and wake Dad, I fantasize. The manhole cover will explode upward, Jett will emerge at street level and dance a victory jig in the storm with Erin, and next they'll come find Trog and me.

Then there's reality, which involves a dog and me in a dark, unknown, half-flooded cave. No one knows where we are, and I don't know how to get us out. The water is rising because of the rain. My legs go weak, and my ears ring like they're inside that fallen church bell. The ceiling and walls seem to close in.

Get it together. You can handle this.

First, I examine the wall behind me for any hollows or passages. Zero.

"Trog, do you swim?" I ask, my light searching the walls on the other side of the stream. I wade into the water up to my hips, every step a cautious foot-plant, the treachery of falling in and being pulled downstream all but strangling my breath.

Trog barks and refuses to follow. Oh-oh. But it's not like I can force him. On the other side of the stream, the mud is calf deep. The way it sucks on each and every stride, I'm waging a battle to make forward progress. Finally, I reach the far wall and examine every dank nook and cranny, looking for a route that continues. None have an air current, and none of the ones large enough to step into go very far. The tormenting assemblage of false tunnels is messing with my mind. It's as if this were once a Roman amphitheatre surrounded by stately statues that have long since disappeared, leaving only the pedestals in arched nooks they once occupied.

What if I leap into the stream and let it take me where it will? Nope. My light indicates it disappears into a cylindrical hole just large enough to accommodate a slithering serpent. I'd smash my head, get swallowed and stuck in its throat, and drown. And the upstream source? A pipe-sized tunnel that maybe Jett, Dad, and I can explore when the water lowers, but right now it'd be like trying to stick our heads into a firehose spurting full strength.

I wade back across the stream, pat Trog, and sink to the ground, defeated. I'll die down here, I think, my bones joining those from the church collapse. I won't get to hear Erin and Jett report on the green dye. If only all the time I wasted chasing the Door could have been applied to helping Dad finish and share our maps for the community's safety instead of to an immature pursuit of fame. If only Mica and I had worked together.

In fact, though, Mica wouldn't have tried breaking into Dad's safe if the two of us had resolved our stupid quarrel long ago. Two stubborn, over-prideful cavers. If only I'd believed him earlier this week when he said he was ready to collaborate.

What did Erin tell me? *People have power over you only if you give them permission to.*

Pride comes before a fall. For cavers, literally.

Trog nudges me. I take his giant head in my arms and bury my face in his neck. "I'm sorry, Trog. I don't know how to save us." Not before the rainstorm fills this place up or collapses the ceiling.

My gloom almost causes me to miss a silent but significant event. A swirly, fluorescent-green line flows past me like a school of radioactive eels. I lift my light just in time to witness the phenomenon.

"Erin, you did it," I mutter, trying to generate the enthusiasm this should spark. "I hereby baptize this cave 'Nettles,'" I announce to no one, "given all the nettles at its entrance hole. And I declare it is a missing link in the chain of caves on our map".

But it doesn't mean Trog and I won't die trying to find our way out.

CHAPTER TWENTY-THREE

"Hudson!" Ana shouts as a powerful searchlight blinds me. "Hudson, are you down here? Are you okay?"

Trog leaps out of my arms and rockets to her, knocking her over and licking her face as I pull myself to my feet.

I must be seeing things. Why would she be down here? How did she get here? Did she tumble in too?

"Are you hurt?" she asks, placing her hands gently on my shoulders and focusing her green eyes on my face. Our eyes lock, my heart pounds, and my body tingles at her touch, but only for a moment before I remember she's a traitor and step away. "No, I'm not hurt. Trog and I are both okay. How'd you find us? How'd you get here? Do you know how to get out?"

"We're here to get you out," she says, her fingers running down my neck.

"We?"

"Mica and I."

My teeth grind.

"He's up top, waiting with a rope."

She moves her beam from my face to the surrounding walls and fantastic formations. Scanning the cave slowly, respectfully, she shakes her head in amazement. "I forgot how beautiful caves can be. I miss caving, Hudson. This region must be full of jewels like this."

I don't reply, anxious to get out of here.

"Trog took off panicked when the thunder and lightning started," she says. "I was chasing after him when I saw the two of you disappear. Your bike and the mudhole confirmed I wasn't imagining things. I ran to get a rescue rope, helmet, and light from Mica, who insisted on helping. How'd you find this place, anyway? And what happened—Trog followed you in?" She frowns at my bike helmet and sneakers, which she must know I'd never wear caving.

"No, the sinkhole opened up when I was freeing Trog's leash and paw from some barbed wire."

"Barbed wire again?" She leans down and examines Trog head to toe. "Have you noticed that wherever someone puts up barbed wire, a few days later workers come and fill in that gap with cement or gravel or stones?" she says.

I say nothing. I hadn't noticed that, but am not about to retort, *I'm sure your father knows all about it.*

"Mica was saying it's been appearing all over the place," she continues. "Someone's messing with the exits—the resurgences— around here. You're shivering." She pulls an emergency blanket from the mud-covered pack I hadn't noticed she was wearing and steps closer to wrap it around me.

The warmth is welcome, and as she arranges it slowly, gently, she pulls me toward her and brushes her lips against mine.

Conflicted, I pull away. "Did you tell Mica about the manhole?"

Illuminated by the searchlight in her lowered hand, she looks hurt and startled. "Of course not."

I make my voice harsh. "Erin said you did." Then guilt packs a punch as I realize that Erin never actually said that. At the Jukebox before we joined the protest, she just said, "*They're in here a lot lately, those two.*"

Ana looks thoughtful. "Well, I didn't, but if Erin said so, you know why, don't you?"

"No."

"She's got it bad for you, Hudson."

I think back to how Erin propped the door open so that I could see Ana and Mica together, like she wanted me to see Ana wasn't worth my time.

"You never called me about the movie. Because of your dad, I guess?" Ana brings me back to now, hanging back and studying me.

"My dad needs a lot of care, so I haven't had time to think of anything else," I reply. "Plus, I thought—Erin made me think—you and Mica?"

A smile spreads slowly across her face, and she shakes her head. "No." She moves closer, embraces me, and plants a long kiss on my lips, which I find myself returning. If I was shivering before, I'm warming up fast now. Trog barks and leaps up to separate us, which makes us laugh and breaks the spell.

"Mica's waiting," she whispers, and slides her arm around my waist to walk me to the hole. "Now that you've found an entrance to this place, he wants you and me to help him calculate the danger factor in here," she says, sweeping her hand around the cave. "To make sure it doesn't turn into a sinkhole."

"Can't do that without a set of transponders or 185-megahertz cave radios to triangulate," I say in a voice that sounds steady, even if I feel turned upside down and inside out by conflicting emotions.

"Yes, we can," she insists, cocking an eyebrow. "There are low-tech solutions too."

I halt, swing her around, and put my face up to hers. "You'd seriously help us do a proper investigation?"

"Anything to get you two caving idiots talking again," she says, smoothing my mud-coated hair out of my eyes. "Is it okay for me to like both of you, but not Mica in that way?"

"What if your dad catches you helping us?"

"I'll be grounded for 150 years and probably given a 'manicure' involving pins shoved under my fingernails." Her laughter fills the dark stadium. "But you can't keep a caver above-ground forever, and you guys are onto something important."

"I didn't take you for such a rebel," I say, sweeping her off her feet and carrying her giggling toward the Nettle Slide.

As I set her down again, her face goes serious. "If we hadn't found you, how would you have gotten out?"

I take her searchlight from her and cast it around. "I've named this Nettle Cave. It's clearly under the community centre, and near the Big One sinkhole, but way closer to the surface. None of those dark spaces over there turns into a passage that goes anywhere. If you hadn't found me, I'd have had to crawl through either the Serpent Squeeze"—I use the light to highlight the small cylindrical stream-exit at the end of the cave—"or the Firehose Funnel." I spotlight the stream entry at the other end. "And no, I have no idea if or where either goes." But maybe I'll have more of an idea after talking to Erin and Jett.

"Why do I get the feeling you like naming caves and passages?" she says.

"My favourite part," I reply with a wink. "Now let's do the Nettle Slide rope tow."

A shout from above urges us to the hole's bottom, where ropes are hanging.

Ana cups her hands around her mouth and calls up, "We're here and no one's injured!"

"Ladies first," Mica responds.

I notice mud dribbling down the slide's walls like melting wax on a candle and hear the continued pounding of rain.

"I'm no lady," Ana retorts, smiling at me and grabbing the ropes. "We're Search and Rescue, Mica Brown!"

CHAPTER TWENTY-FOUR

Mica and I are leaning over maps, our legs dangling over the keystone rock on the bridge beneath Ribbon Falls. We're wary of each other. It has taken time to agree to talk. But it's vaguely starting to feel like the old days.

"I'm sorry for ghosting you this past year," Mica says, studying the stone edge of the bridge. "I panicked when the landslide blocked my entrance, and I guess it was easier to blame you than admit I was guilty of exploring without you. I was also really tired of all our arguing. It'd stopped being fun. We're too much alike, you know. Way competitive." He grins weakly.

"You're right about that," I say, "and I'm sorry too. Turned out I kind of enjoyed teaming up with my dad more, once you went rogue, and Jett has proven his stripes bigtime."

"Agreed, from what I've heard. Look forward to caving with him sometime."

"I… miss Dad." I toss pieces of bark after the pebbles Mica is dropping into the stream.

"I miss your dad too," Mica says quietly. "I hope he has a full recovery."

"Me too."

"I wonder what happened with our dads all those years ago. Does your dad ever talk about it?" Mica asks. "Mine won't. He also won't say a thing about caves he explored when he was young. All he has ever said is that he lost interest in caving and let your dad keep all the maps."

"I've always wondered why they stopped being friends, why your dad stopped caving, and why my dad ended up with the maps. I've seen old photos of them grinning at the camera in their caving gear. Once or twice, when I've gotten Dad in a good mood, he'll light up about his adventures with your father. They were tight caving buddies back in the day. It was after the Big One they fell apart. And he definitely won't talk about that. What do you think happened after the Big One?"

Mica shrugs. "Had to have been pretty traumatic, your dad losing his father, mine his grandfather. That's definitely when my dad stopped caving. Guess it just put him off.

"We'll talk this out more," Mica promises, "but for now, we've agreed to do what we do best together."

"Yes," I acknowledge, feeling lighter than I have for a while. "Cave exploration, but this time with a higher purpose, which we can't do without following safety rules. So, yesterday's green dye proved that from here, the stream runs into Aladdin I Cave, then through some mystery spaces to Firehose Funnel and Nettle Cave, then down Serpent's Squeeze. From there, we're not sure, but it seems like it runs through some mystery passage and into Tass Bay, passing by the Bell Wall on an elbow-turn so sharp that the dye leaked just a little through the cracks there."

"Yep," Mica says. "And that re-routing is why the manhole culvert and T-Rex, as you call it, is dry. And you believe me—I've never been near, let alone through, T-Rex, which was somehow diverted long ago, naturally or unnaturally."

"So, you've never, ever been through the manhole?"

"Never. Seems stupid we didn't think of it before, but then again, the manhole was cemented over."

"Exactly."

"Well, first we need to anchor a rope at the top of Nettle Slide and drop down to get some photos and readings on the walls and ceiling of the place," Mica says, "maybe with help from someone standing in the community centre. That'll get us crucial info we can take to Dad and Mr. Toop."

"Readings they may not want."

"True. But once we make that info public, they'll be forced to do something."

"Maybe they'll close the community centre and get a real inspector to look at it, and stop some of TT's activities," I say.

"What TT activities?"

"The undercover clearcutting near Aladdin I and the road built to haul the lumber out from there. We should maybe go up and take pictures of all that."

"That's trespassing," says Mr. Williams, making us jump. "Hi, boys," he adds as he rounds a curve in the path and halts. He's smiling, his hands settled on the straps of his oversize pack.

How much did he overhear? Can we trust him?

"Sorry, wasn't eavesdropping. Just happened to hear you as I was huffing up this trail. It's steep for an out-of-shape guy like me."

"Hi, Mr. Williams," Mica and I say at the same time, rising slowly to our feet.

"How's your father, Hudson?"

"Recovering, thanks."

"Good. From the little bit I heard just now, sounds like you two are on the right track. It's especially good to see the mayor's son on the right side of things." He looks at Mica, who squirms a little. "I just want to point out that the ill-advised clearcutting to which you're referring is on TT land. They've installed a number of guards, and now cameras. I know this because I've already snuck in there and gotten photos. In fact, I'll be showing them at a community meeting I've booked for tomorrow. You'll join us, I hope?"

"Of course. It's on our calendars," I say. Hope the meeting stays peaceful.

"Three o'clock at the community centre. There's something else I want to talk to you two about."

"Shoot," Mica says.

"Some fishermen were telling me that they saw a streak of green in Tass Bay yesterday. It appeared, then dispersed. Not natural phosphorescence, but a phenomenon they'd never seen before. They thought I might know, being a scientist."

"Where in Tass Bay, exactly?" I ask, trying to hide my excitement.

"So, it is something to do with you two?" His face has gone stern, and I have to remind myself we're not in class and he's not even our teacher anymore. "I've heard about cavers using tracer dye, but I don't like to think you'd risk that in our pristine watershed."

"It's nontoxic, Mr. Williams. Guaranteed. Where exactly did they see it?"

"I'll tell you if you promise not to do it again. We're having enough problems with TT policies negatively affecting the aquifer, boys, as you'll hear at tomorrow's meeting."

"We won't do it again," I say quickly. We don't need to, anyway.

"It was just off the pebble beach immediately below the Jukebox. I don't know what-all you two are up to, Mica and Hudson, but cave exploration is not safe at the best of times, and with town officials and townspeople riled up these days, there are additional dangers. Please be smart and careful."

"We are," Mica responds. "So, are you going to stay living in Tass, Mr. Williams? Will you be back teaching in the fall?"

Mr. Williams straightens his shoulders, and his eyes seem to twinkle. "No more teaching for me, boys. I'm starting a new business. Can't tell you about it yet, but let's just say I've discovered my inner entrepreneur. And yes, I will stay here in lovely Tass."

"Cool," I say, curious—but also anxious to get back to Mica's and my private conference.

"Have a good summer, boys," our ex-teacher says, and off he walks, hiking stick poking into the dirt, pack sagging off his shoulders.

"That guy's a pure-water fanatic," Mica comments.

"Well, maybe that's what Tass needs," I say. "Interesting he snuck in to get photos. Combined with the ones we're going to get, that meeting could get lively."

"Yeah, speaking of which, let's get back to business." Mica looks around as if to make sure there are no more eavesdropping hikers.

"You going to tell your dad about what we're up to before Mr. Williams's meeting?" I ask.

"Nah. Things are bad enough between Dad and me. He doesn't want me caving anymore." Mica picks up a handful of pebbles and tosses them forcefully into the stream, which is down to a trickle after the rainstorm. "As if he can stop me."

I unfold our maps, a proud new compilation of his and mine.

"We're still missing stuff," Mica grumbles.

"Places where there be dragons."

"Places you'd think our dads would have discovered when they were caving together."

"Before the Big One," I note sadly.

"Yeah."

A breeze ruffles the maps like ghostly fingers are messing with us. I shiver and look about, fighting off a sense of being haunted again.

"What I don't get," I say, "is how all the past year, Dad was steering Jett and me into caves away from where the green dye just told us was the Castle-Dungeon border. Coincidentally or purposefully? Just before we discovered Pool Dome, he gave us this whole speech: 'It's highly unlikely the two systems connect, as I've told you over and over again.'"

"Sounds like your dad."

"When Jett and I pushed for exploring the manhole, Dad insisted there was nothing to pursue there. Definitely not a go, he said. And of course we believed him. Even before that, he always refused to look for cave entrances under the graveyard, out of respect the dead. And not long ago, when we were at the Aladdin I/II junction, trying to decide which to explore first, Dad chose Aladdin I, even though it's clear now that Aladdin II would have taken us closer to the border."

I flash back to an earlier conversation.

"What does the secret Door smell like?" Jett joked.

Dad rolls his eyes. I fist-bump Jett as we study our fearless leader. Dad leans his face into one passage, then the other, turning his cheek as if waiting for a kiss. What he is doing, of course, is waiting for his cheek to feel air current. Which passage has a wisp of air current, the indication of a possible exit? My judgment says the left one.

Dad smiles and jerks his head to the right. We stumble after him without arguing.

"Aladdin I is so obviously in upper Castle territory," I say. "The Door always had to be in town, or maybe that's 20/20 hindsight."

"Your dad was never into the Door," Mica reminds me, stuffing the maps into his pack. "He was all about mapmaking."

A sudden thought makes me jump up so fast I almost fall off the bridge. "Maybe both our dads have been down the manhole, been in Nettle Cave, and know the route between. Maybe they've been steering us away from ever finding the Door."

"For what reason, Huds?"

I think for a moment. "Respect for the bell, the bones, the history, the townspeople who died."

"Hmm."

"When I was little, I remember Mom making herself and me a picnic and walking us up to the memorial garden, picnic basket swinging. I was excited. We were halfway through eating when Dad appeared, looking really upset, and all but yanked Mom off the grounds. I can still see him whipping the picnic blanket off the grass, and it blowing out of his hands in the wind, and him chasing it with tears in his eyes. Mom followed him and hugged him a really long time, like he needed calming down or something. When she finally noticed me clinging to her knees, she wrapped us all in the picnic blanket and included me in the family hug. But she never, ever explained what was actually going on that day. I think in Dad's mind, Mom and I were trivializing sacred ground or something. I'm sure it had to do with the tragedy of losing his father there."

"That's pretty heavy."

"It was right after that he started making the model church. I remember Mom bringing home some of the materials and acting like she was all interested in it."

We both go silent.

"So you think maybe our dads found the bell while caving one day?" Mica asks. "Except you said whoever broke a stalagmite in T-Rex and scratched lines on the Bell Wall was super skinny. That's neither of our dads."

"Not today," I state. "But we're talking twenty years ago. The old photos show them way skinnier." Why hadn't that occurred to me before now?

"What was scratched on the wall? Like, Morse code or something?"

"A circle. A rectangle. A trapezoid."

"Okay, that's weird. A caveman giving his kids lessons on geometric shapes. Tell me more."

"The rectangle was inside the circle. The trapezoid was at the bottom. The trapezoid reminded me of a big fireplace."

"A rectangle inside a circle is a 'Do not enter' symbol."

My heartbeat races. "Huh."

"A trapezoid doesn't make any sense."

"You know who'd know?" I ask, gripping Mica's wrist. "My dad. Follow me!"

Fifteen minutes later we burst through the front door of my house, startling my mother, who's pulling cookies from the oven.

"Yum, thanks Mom," I greet her, swiping a few.

"Hi, Mica," she says, looking surprised and pleased. "Help yourself, boys!"

"How's Dad? How are things? Hey, these are really good." I try to sound casual.

"Thanks, and he's having a good day," she says, raising an eyebrow. "What are you two up to? You're wanting something, I presume?" She kisses the top of my head before I can stop her.

"Mom, do you know the code for Dad's safe?"

She straightens up and looks at me. "I don't. You could try asking your father. Why do you want to know? There's nothing in there but old maps, you know."

"I know," I call back as I take the stairs two at a time, Mica at my heels mumbling thanks to Mom through a spray of cookie crumbs.

The room is dim, with one beam of light from a broken blind highlighting the church model. Mica, though he has seen it many times before, touches its steeple gently.

"Dad?" I whisper.

His eyelids flutter up and he smiles at Mica and me. He has been way more alert and almost cheerful lately, which gives me the courage to get right to the point.

"Dad, I've never asked you this before, but would you tell me the combination for the safe in the den? We really need to check any maps you have in there."

Eyes narrowed, he shakes his head vigorously.

"Dad, we think the community centre is in danger of sinking into a cave beneath it. We're going into that cave this afternoon to get some readings and photographs so we can talk TT into pausing their operations and closing the centre and doing new inspections. It would help us to know what's on each side of the cave under the community centre. We don't have time to do all the exploring it would take to fill in the blanks on the maps we have. You have some you've never shown me, am I right?"

He heaves a sigh, appears to process all that for several long seconds, and finally nods in a resigned sort of way. "S-s-so."

"Yes, Dad. We know. I've been down the manhole and dived into the sump. I found the bell and bones embedded in that wall accessed from the manhole. There's no need to hide things from us anymore. I'm sorry you can't help us physically, but can you please trust us?"

Dad is now silent, eyes closed.

"Behh," he says.

I sit straight up, and Mica leans down close to his face.

"Behh." His arm shoots up and accidentally connects with my ear.

"Ouch! What's he saying, Mica? He's trying to tell us something."

"Bell," comes my mother's voice from the bedroom doorway. "I think he's trying to say 'bell.'"

"Yes, Dad, the collapsed church's bell. I know you didn't want—"

"Behh." His arm comes up again and his index finger points to the ceiling, then leans left like a moving searchlight.

"The bell in the church tower!" Mica's voice trembles with excitement as he moves closer to Dad's side table. "Here, this church! The model!"

Dad nods his head yes, his body relaxing a little.

"Let me help you," says Mom. "I've always known the bell tower—the steeple—disconnects, but I've had no reason to touch it for years." She tugs gently and it lifts. A yellowed piece of paper rests inside. Mom plucks it out, looks to Dad for approval, then hands it to me.

"Thanks, Dad," I say, my voice hitching.

He lowers his hand onto my head and rests it there like he's blessing me. I squeeze his hand, hug Mom, and then Mica and I dash into the den, where Mica insists on reading out the numbers as I twirl the dial.

CHAPTER TWENTY-FIVE

It's midnight of a sticky-hot night and twelve hours before Operation Nettle, so sleep is not happening for me. I rise and part the curtains of my bedroom window to look out on Tass at the witching hour, then raise the window and stick my head out.

It's peaceful, still, and dark, with twinkling stars and wisps of fog that rise from the dampened soil of yesterday's rain. There's also a light breeze, the kind that beckons from a cave entrance. The moving air will soon disperse the mist, but not before I roam the streets to commune with my favourite town at its darkest, richest time of day.

I pull on my clothes, tiptoe down the stairs, and close the front door silently after me. Flashlight in hand, I amble toward Main Street, where pools of light beneath all twelve of Tass's streetlights swirl like blotted watercolours in the ghostly quiet.

Hopefully we can use our maps to help save the town from a sinkhole disaster, but right now, the passages are all ours—mine, Dad's, Jett's, Mica's, and a handful of others. The hidden hollows pose risks, yes, but my dad has taught me well: Knowledge and a respect for science reduce those risks, as I wish TT would figure out.

As Dad likes to say, science and the truth win out every time—in the end.

The noise of an approaching car snaps me out of my daydream. I step back into the shadows of a bush across the street from Tass Gas. The station is closed, of course, so whatever lost tourist has ended up in this end-of-the-road community at this hour will soon figure out the pumps don't open again till 10:00 a.m.

In the wavering vapour and weak light, an expensive-looking sedan turns right, proceeds one block farther, and stops on a side street. A large man in rubber boots and work clothes steps out. He glances about in a wary manner, then walks to the rear of the vehicle to pop open the trunk.

Okay, not trying to get gas. Just parking there. I watch suspiciously as he manhandles out first a wheelbarrow, then a bag so heavy he's grunting, and finally a short-handled tool that looks like a stunted hoe. Finally, he lifts out a container of water, eye goggles, and heavy-duty gloves. In no time, he has parked the wheelbarrow in the centre of the road—really?—and slit the bag to spill its contents into the barrow. Soon he's adding water and stroking the mixture with the tool till it looks like lumpy oatmeal. *What the—*?

It's when he starts dumping lumps of the oatmeal on the manhole cover, then smoothing it out, that I leap out of hiding and start shouting. "Don't you dare block that manhole cover!"

He jumps back and stares at me.

"Where'd you come from, Young Greer? Past your curfew, isn't it?" It's Mr. Toop himself, using the sweet-talking tone he used on Mom while trying to get to her sign that contract. Instinctively I take a step back. But my fists clench.

"What, you can't get workers to do your dirty work for you, so now you're sneaking around in the middle of the night yourself?" Did I actually just say that to my parents' boss and sort-of-girlfriend's father?

He narrows his eyes but continues stroking the mix and slopping it on top of the cover, one eye trained on me.

I pull myself up to my full height. "Don't close off that cover."

"Or what?" Mr. Toop asks with a hearty laugh. "Mayor's orders, kid. It was closed up years ago, and the concrete just needs refreshing."

"In the middle of the night?" I say sarcastically. "By the VP of TT?"

"Do yourself a favour and go home, Hudson," Mr. Toop says, slinging an over-thick layer on the iron lid. *He doesn't even know how to apply concrete.* "Or better yet, help us out by giving up those maps you think are so important, so we can close more entrances into dangerous places. Otherwise, someone's going to get hurt. Your mother would probably like those entries sealed up. I suspect she worries about you."

"Leave my mom out of this. You know you're endangering the community by ignoring scientific facts and pulling stunts like this."

Mr. Toop goes red-faced and raises his hoe like a spear. I continue to stand there, given that I honestly don't expect it to come sailing at me. Which is why, if I hadn't reacted swiftly, it would have struck my neck.

I may be small, but I'm fast and strong. I duck just in time, dash over to upend the entire barrow, and thrust its handles into his chest. The concrete mix pours out onto his legs and shoes. He roars, and the two of us charge at each other like bull and bullfighter. Soon we're spinning in the wet concrete, punching and bashing, the granular grey substance coating our hair, dribbling into our ears. Lucky for me the hoe is no longer within his reach.

"Leave my daughter alone, you brat," he says between gasps. "You're a lunatic!"

"Leave our community alone," I rasp back before a punch in the nose sends shots of pain through my skull and turns the concrete pink. "Leave our caves alone before you get someone killed. Like Ana."

He freezes in mid-punch and seems to come to his senses. I take the opportunity to roll all the way to the far curb, where I curl into a ball.

When he makes no move to follow, I stand and pour liquid from my water bottle all over myself, well aware of what havoc liquid concrete can wreak, especially on eyes and exposed skin. I'm also busy calculating. It takes a long time for concrete to dry. Once Mr. Toop leaves, it'll be easy enough to smash through with a crowbar from my dad's garage. I'll undo Mr. Toop's efforts before his sedan reaches his driveway.

Across the street, Mr. Toop rises, tosses everything back into the wheelbarrow, does a token smoothing-stomp on his mess, and somehow manages to get all his stuff back onto the tarp protecting the inner sanctum of his sedan.

"Job's done," he snaps. "Get out of here before I call the cops on you, Hudson Greer."

"I'm shaking in my boots," I say, backing into the shadows, "while yours are turning into concrete. And you bluff as poorly as you close up manholes or run a logging company. Sir." The last few words are flung his way from a high-speed sprint home.

CHAPTER TWENTY-SIX

Five of us—Mica, me, Jett, Dirk, and Don—are sitting at a pink Formica-topped table in the Jukebox, waiting for Ana as we chow down on fries. I wave at Erin as she wipes down empty tables.

She smiles and calls over, "Are you all going to the community centre meeting at three?"

"We are," I reply, making a mental note to suggest a walk with her one of these days, to clear the air between us. I'll try not to hurt her feelings.

Will Ana show like she promised? Her dad wouldn't dare tell her about our incident last night. I'm counting on that.

"Dirk and Don," Mica addresses his guys like someone has appointed him Chief of Underground Operations. "Proud of you two. And you're clear on your assignment in this, right?"

"We're going to take one of the avalanche beacons into the community centre before people start setting up there this afternoon, turn it on to 'Receive,' and wait for the signal that may come from yours where you are below us," says Dirk.

"In other words, we pretend you're a victim under the snow and listen for the beep-beeps that go every second," Don asserts brightly, dipping a fry into ketchup.

"Are you sure avalanche beacons work through rock?" Don asks.

I wonder if the two are half relieved to have gotten out of sliding down a mud hole into a cave that may be in danger of collapsing.

"They don't usually," Mica replies. "Depends on the rock type, and how thick the slab is. You'll get a signal only if the slab is no chunkier than 1.7 metres, an average human's height. That's a dangerously thin crust between a building's foundations and a cave's ceiling and may indicate serious erosion over the years."

"Over the years or in recent months from TT work," I add grimly. "You're there just in case a signal goes through."

"Then we come out and help you guys up the rope at Nettle Slide," Don recites. "Then we all go different directions to throw people off, but all meet where we agreed and with the tools we've stashed nearby."

"After that job," Mica says, "we can go to the community centre meeting. You're both crucial to this operation, you know, and we appreciate it."

The two squirm a little, heads held high.

"Thanks, Don, for lending us your family's avalanche beacons," Mica adds.

He grins. "What they don't know can't hurt them."

"Is Ana bringing special walkie-talkies that work through rock?" Jett asks, drumming his fingers on the table beside his plate. "Or those transponder things that look like metal detectors and send radio signals?"

"Nope, no one around here has anything that expensive and specialized," I reply.

"That's why we settled for the avalanche beacons," Mica explains.

"Then how will we know if you're in trouble and we need to come after you?" Dirk sounds like his hero-complex is half eager for that to happen.

"We'll knock three times on the cave ceiling. You'll hear it through the community centre floor," I joke.

D-squared smirks. Jett waves to Ana as she enters with—

"Whose birthday?" Dirk demands, arms crossed in front of his chest. "Is there cake involved too?"

I grin. She's wearing orange coveralls and carrying a Happy Birthday helium balloon. Of course! A low-tech way to measure the height of the cave ceiling. Tucked under one arm is a dinged-up yellow caving helmet, and her waist-pack looks suspiciously bulky, but I won't ask yet what's in it. Her heavy leather boots look like they've done business in many a cave before. She has her gloves on already. In other words, she's even more gorgeous than usual.

"Hi, everyone. Nice of you to be part of this," she says, her voice dropping to a whisper even though no one's within earshot. "Now, everyone leaves here separately and scatters so we don't look suspicious in case there are any TT spies around, right?"

"Sure you aren't one of them?" Dirk needles her.

Ana just turns a high-beam smile on him and Don, then nods to Mica, Jett, and me. We exit one at a time and head in different directions. As I leave, I wave at Erin and say, "Save some lemonade. We'll be back in an hour."

"I know you're all going caving, duh," she says from where she's washing dishes. A moment later, she pokes her head out the door. "Be careful!"

The four of us undergrounders meet up ten minutes later at Nettle Slide, where Mica has already laid the rope anchor. We look about. Not a soul in sight. Just a bulldozer starting up noisily over at what's left of the TT parking lot. My nails press into my palms as I reflect on how Dad should be that guy. Or standing here with me, arm around my shoulder.

Downhill, D-squared lope up to the community centre, hands stuffed in their pockets, acting like they're in no hurry.

"Good job on the rope, Mica," Ana says, testing the anchor. "Let's make like firefighters down a pole." She disappears down the rope like a pro. Soon only the balloon floats over the hole until, with one tug, it disappears downward too.

I swallow, look at Mica and Jett, and don my helmet, switching on its headlamp. I grab the rope and climb down. Next thing I know, my boots touch firm ground far below.

"Whoa, awesome formations," Mica observes as he lands lightly on his feet behind me.

"Serious booty," Jett whispers reverently.

Ana is duct-taping an avalanche beacon on top of the balloon, from which a couple of measuring tapes stapled end-to-end (to make a super long one) dangles. She releases it, and we all count to four before it hits the ceiling. Peeps from the device indicate that it's talking with Jett and team, which is not good.

"Crap," Mica says. "That slab is razor thin."

"Iffy," I agree, pressing my fingernails into my palms. "Too bad we can't ride up under the balloon and examine if there are cracks growing."

"Doesn't work that way," Ana informs us. "Rocks aren't like concrete. They don't crack gradually to offer warning. They just—"

A crash like the sound of glass breaking sounds behind us. I picture a greenhouse hit by meteors.

We stare at the stalactite that just let loose from the roof and fell like a giant glass dagger. Its shattered remains are scattered across the floor, some at our feet. Come to think of it, there are a few rock slabs and boulders on the ground that weren't here on my last visit.

Ana steps forward to clutch the balloon "string" with shaking hands. She reads the numbers dragging on the floor. "This cave is five metres high, roughly one and a half storeys," she says solemnly. "And evidently unstable."

"But we came to do a job," I say through gritted teeth as I pull out Dad's "toys": compass, clinometer, and laser rangefinder.

I aim the rangefinder at the far wall, a red dot pinging to reveal the length of our space. In short order, I've measured the width as well. "Nettle Cave is roughly thirty metres square, like a domed stadium," I say.

Ana, after tugging down the balloon and releasing the avalanche beacon from it, unzips her waist-pack and produces a drone. A cheap little one like kids have.

I shake my head in amazement. "For photographing the ceiling. Genius."

"Exactly," she says. "Don't you dare tell my dad which of us took the photos when we present them in a few hours." Soon the cave is filled with the sound of the drone's whine as it snaps photos of the walls, roof, and boulder-strewn floor. As it photographs the floor, I note that the stream that rushed through on my last visit is barely a trickle today.

"Now what?" Jett asks, gazing warily overhead, probably fearful of more dropping stalactites.

Mica opens his mouth and says something, but his words are drowned out by a roar, bang, and metallic clash from the top of Nettle Slide. Instinctively taking a step back, I see and feel the rumble of two boulders tumbling down the chute, followed by an avalanche of other rocks. One bounces and slams into Mica's knee. He screams and falls to the ground, writhing.

"Mica!" I run over to him and inspect bloody gashes on his

kneecap. My stomach turns sour. "Breathe, Mica. Deep breaths." I scoop my hand into the stream and dribble cold water on the wound, then shout, "First-aid kit, Jett or Ana!"

Jett unzips his pack super-fast and fishes one out as Ana stays frozen in place like a statue of a girl holding a balloon.

"Ana, bring me that balloon!" Jett orders. "Huds, help me pull Mica back from the slide!"

I don't need a second order as our entrance hole clogs up with a thunderous rain of rubble, more spilling into the cave toward our feet.

Ana coughs as she backs up with the balloon in her arms. Mica, who normally sucks up pain better than anyone I know, is alternately howling and gasping as Jett and I drag him to safety. All four of us retreat like soldiers under fire. I find the din of the slide's cave-in so deafening that I have to cover my ears. But it's not a cave-in, is it?

"TT's backfilling the hole for safety," Jett guesses as he starts dabbing alcohol pads on Mica's wounds and duct-taping the balloon into place as a cushion.

"What do we do, Hudson?" Ana asks with a shiver.

Mica looks up to me from the cave floor, eyes blinking rapidly.

Just then, the aftershocks of the rock-fill activity unloose two house-sized chunks of the ceiling on the other side of the cave. One of them, to my horror, falls across Firehose Funnel's portal. No! That's two of our three exits now gone!

CHAPTER TWENTY-SEVEN

The boulder blocking Firehose Funnel looks way too big to push away, even with three able-bodied cavers, and I don't want to hang out in here any longer anyway.

"The Serpent Squeeze!" I shout. "Jett, lift Mica up under his other shoulder. Ana, follow me!"

Jett and I carry Mica to the far end and ease him down gently in front of the small tubular passage.

"Even without a messed-up knee, I'll never fit," says Mica, forehead sweaty, body shaking.

Jett persuades him to drink from a water bottle and hands him some aspirin.

"Me neither, Huds," Jett says gravely. "But you and Ana are small enough to squeeze through and go fetch us help."

"I won't leave without you," I say, vaguely aware that the noise at the now plugged-up Nettle chute has stopped and nothing else is shaking loose from walls or ceiling. We turn and stare as Ana slips off her boots and coveralls. Standing there before us in shorts and T, she whips out a Swiss Army knife and slices up one leg of her caving outfit.

"Mica needs more layers. We don't want him to go into shock," she says as she gently slips Mica into the protective clothing.

Hearing my buddy's teeth chatter, I'm quick to help her.

"Rule of Three," Ana states, giving me a stern look. "One to stay behind if someone is injured while another goes for help.

In this case, that's you or me going for help. Or both of us. Jett's right. We're the smallest. Mica and Jett wait here."

I sigh. "Okay, but we have three geologist's hammers, right? Jett, take yours and start making this opening bigger. That'll help whatever medics we can send back to you. According to Dad's maps, the passage widens quickly ahead and stays reasonably roomy. But you should also know it keeps plunging down so far that your ears may pop."

"Your dad's maps?" Ana echoes.

"Hopefully we'll have medics in the passage by the time you widen this entrance throat."

"Where does it lead?" Jett asks, checking our patient's pulse.

I look to Mica, who is clenching his teeth.

"To a small room with a sump and a wall with a high window."

"And an iron bell embedded in the wall," Mica adds tersely.

Ana's eyes all but bug out.

"Don't try to climb up to the window," I instruct. "The wall will crumble on you. Around the corner from the sump is a natural culvert that feeds out into Tass Bay below the Jukebox, but it's a sieve of stone with absolutely no way through, according to Dad's written instructions." My voice sounds grim, even to me.

"Good to know," Jett says.

"Then how do we get out of the little room you're talking about?" Ana sounds a bit choked.

"Trust us," a pale-faced Mica replies before I can, being the only other one who has seen Dad's yellowed map from the safe. "Huds has our backs."

"Ana, you're following right behind me," I order.

"Okay," she says, face going a little pale. "We'll fit, right?"

"Where your helmet can go, your body can follow," I quote

a caving motto before removing my helmet and thrusting it into the dark cavity. There's a hair's width of space between its edges and the walls. I shiver.

She leans forward, kisses me right in front of everyone, pulls her boots back on, and ties her waist-pack to them. "See you soon," she says to Jett and Mica, and drops to the floor behind me like someone has ordered her to do push-ups.

Helmet back on tight, light switched on, I navigate forward through a squeeze I've never done before, totally trusting in Dad's old map. It requires me to exhale until I'm almost blue so that I'm skinny enough to fit. It's excruciatingly tight.

"A crazy serpent designed this," I mutter, then fill in the response, "And who's following the crazy serpent?"

Minutes later I feel the vibrations of Jett well behind us clanging on the entrance with the axe. Ana and I have two axes in the waist-packs tied to our feet, packs dragging along behind us like reluctant puppies.

Once, I twist my head back and call out, "You okay, Ana?"

"I'm stuck. Like, stuck solid. Going to have to try and back out."

"No, you're not," I assure her. "You're temporarily detained. Breathe, Ana."

A moment later, "Yeah, maybe I'm okay now, Huds, thanks. It's just been a long time since I've caved, and this is creepy."

"Want me to squirt you with dish soap and pull?"

"As if," comes the muffled reply. "Theoretically, I can't get stuck. I'm smaller than you, Celery Stick."

I guffaw. When did she overhear Mica call me that?

Soon enough, as Dad's map promised, the thin neck widens, and a trace of air current rallies me. It has to be coming from that tiny high window in the Bell Wall, still a long way ahead.

The "down" part continues long and steep. I'm so glad we're not having to share this corkscrew crawl with a stream. Patience, Hudson. Trust Dad. How many years ago did he do this route, map this? After that, it's like he sealed off the route by locking the map in his safe—and was always by my side while caving, to ensure I'd never find the Bell Wall.

Down, down, ever down. To the bowels of unknown Tass. With every passing moment, my craving for more space than this cramped serpent hole grows. Eventually, I burst into the inland side of the Bell Wall room. Its backside. And once again, a sump—the mirror image of the one that haunted me on the other side of the wall—lies at my feet.

As soon as Ana scrambles into the space, I point to the sump. "I'll just be a minute," I say as I plunge in head-first, hands eagerly in front of me, ready to trace the etched lines on this side: the duplicate images of T-Rex's configurations. I mentally name this room T-Rex's Twin. My fingers trace a rectangle inside a circle. Do not enter.

Except in case of emergency, I think.

Pushing myself lower, I feel the trapezoid, the would-be fireplace. But this time my fingers tingle with excitement, because I know its meaning.

Bursting to the surface, I scramble to solid ground and start jumping up and down. "It's there. Get out our geologic axes, girl. We're breaking through the keystone."

"Keystone?"

"After discovering what was deposited down here by the Big One, including the sunken bell, my dad and Mica's dad wanted to seal this place off forever, so they pushed in a tight-fitting slab of rock. It's trapezoid-shaped, just like the keystone on the bridge by Ribbon Falls. The lines that look etched are the borders of the chockstone. We have to smash it up, rip it out. That will create a sizeable opening to T-Rex, the cave with the teeth that leads to the manhole, to get medics in and Mica and Jett out. Mica and I explained all that. Remember?"

"Your dad was here? He knew all along?"

I feel hair rising on the back of my neck as I recall that my grandfather, and Mica's great-grandfather, and an entire congregation of unlucky townspeople are here, an estimated seven storeys beneath where the church once stood. I remember the ghosts flitting about the day I wriggled through T-Rex, and the human bone that came loose in my hand.

"They understand," I say softly. "They're okay with what we need to do to rescue Mica and Jett."

Ana raises an eyebrow. "How thick is this wedge-stone?"

"Too thick for just the two of us. But we're a team of four. I contacted D-squared and they're meeting us the other side with crowbars and—"

Bang! Crunch! comes from the sump, and I leap back. "They're here! Two teams of two, now. We use our axes like crowbars from both sides till it's pried open!"

Ana whips out her axe and plunges into the water bravely, like she's been popping out underwater chock blocks all her life.

Up for breath, down for pushing, twisting, prying. Up for breath… It's a good hour's work, and we have only water bottles and some fruit leather to keep us going.

"We're missing the community centre talk," Ana comments dryly at one point.

"I don't envy your dad trying to go up against Mr. Williams," I say.

"Maybe Mr. Williams will finally persuade him, since I haven't been able to."

"They'll all be wondering where we are," I say, thinking of my mother and father as I sink back into the increasingly cloudy water.

"A chink!" I say the next time we surface. "We'll be able to shake hands with D-squared in a minute!"

"Three helpers the other side!" Ana gasps the next time her head bobs up for oxygen, after peering through the chink. "Dirk, Don, and Erin!"

"Erin?" I echo, stumped. Of course, she followed them. She offered to help. She probably grabbed a crowbar off the Tass Gas guy and can swing one like no one's business when it's about saving lives.

With a series of final swings, our tools touch, the trapezoid crumbles, and the roiled-up waters meet. The hole is now the shape of a palace fireplace. As fine a magic Door as I ever imagined.

Ana and I dive one last time, grab the hands of our colleagues, and pull them through just beneath the lower rim of the bell. Someone brushes up against the clapper; it rings sonorously, three times.

"We did it!" we shout, leaping about on Ana's and my "shore" of the Bell Wall sump, hugging.

The moment of elation is cut short by my informing the group about Mica and Jett. "Ana will explain," I say as I head back into Serpent's Squeeze. "You get a medic down here. I'll get Mica and Jett. We'll all meet up somewhere along here."

What I don't anticipate as I slither upward to help Jett with Mica through the now hopefully enlarged throat is that moments later, Ana and Erin leave D-squared and are on my tail. Yes, Erin—who has never caved before—wriggles through Serpent Squeeze toward Nettle Cave in her bicycle helmet, skirt, and Birkenstock sandals. D-squared doesn't follow. Even if they weren't in charge of fetching medical people, they're both too bulky to fit.

It's a real huff going up, but I'm rewarded by a much less confining exit: The narrow neck has disintegrated.

"Ana? Erin? Everyone okay?" I ask as they wriggle out behind me. I spot Mica and Jett, then swing around.

"We wanted to help," Erin says, feeling Mica's forehead, taking his pulse, and checking his knee bandage. "Nice job, Dr. Jett."

"Thanks," Jett says tiredly.

"You're still okay?" I ask Jett and Mica. Jett is red-faced from the effort of all but smashing the entrance into smithereens.

"Wow, what did that serpent ever do to you?" I kid him, while eyeing Mica closely. He's conscious and no longer shaking, which is a relief. "Mica, you'll fit now, with a little help."

Mica narrows his eyes as I pull out my miniature bottle of dish soap, drip it on him, and start rubbing it around. "Sorry, but you were due for lube service, Mr. Brown. Don't want you temporarily detained on your journey. Only Toothpicks and slim girls get away without it."

"I'll get you back for this," he jokes weakly.

"Jett," I continue, "you're the strongest one here. Now that the entrance is large enough, go in first, feet-first and stomach-down, pull Mica through by the shoulders, and deliver him to Dirk and Don, okay? They'll carry him through the sump and T-Rex and deliver him to an ambulance via the manhole. The rest of us will be right behind you."

"On it, Huds," Jett says. "And don't even think about squirting that on me."

Jett's caving skills have really come along, I note as the pair disappear into the half-obliterated opening.

"Ahem." I address the two ladies. "You were supposed to stay put, but here we are."

"This is way cooler than I imagined," says Erin, following my light as I beam it around the still space. "Now I get it, Huds. Can't believe I advised you to stop caving."

"That was when you were a fortune teller. And you followed the guys down the manhole because…?"

"Don and Dirk came running out of the community centre when they heard that bulldozer, and when I dashed up the hill to see what all the noise was about, they told me what a pickle that put you in and what they were going to do next. We never signalled the driver. It was too late.

"They headed for the manhole," she continues, "and I followed to see if I could help. They didn't get too mad when I trailed them down the manhole. I figured out why you named that place T-Rex, Hudson. I had no idea that kind of stuff was right underneath our town! So cool! Then, the guys shortened one of the teeth for them to get through, even though I could've fit through without that. And they figured out I can hold my breath longer than them, and I can whack a wall pretty good. So, we took turns ramming that underwater block—and, well, you know the rest, ta da!"

I'm trying not to laugh at her enthusiasm. Ana's smiling, too, but with backward glances over her shoulder.

"Erin, Hudson," she says, "it's time to get out of here."

Erin has her head and half her body stuffed into the hole

when we're hit by an explosion like a locomotive engine running through the cave. Sharp debris pelts us from every angle. Rocks rain down, swords plunge from the ceiling, and fine dust fills our nostrils until we're gasping for breath. I find myself with one arm pushing Ana to the ground and the other covering Erin's ankles, knowing in my gut what disaster is unfolding. Screams and falling bodies fill the air.

CHAPTER TWENTY-EIGHT

Only when the cave stops trembling and the onslaught of torpedoing rubble dies away do I dare to open my eyes, look, and listen from where I've been knocked to the floor, half atop Ana. We're trapped in a war zone, a temple of terror.

Human wailing fills the stadium, punctuated by the dull clang-clang of a bell. It's like I've died and joined the congregation.

But the fast-paced peal sounds too much like the firehall's emergency bell. And it's not tomb-dark where I am. There's a patch of sky high overhead.

Meanwhile, there's a human being beneath me squirming out from under.

"Hudson?" Ana says. "Hudson, are you okay?"

An anthill is full of tunnels and cavities, I remember Mr. Williams saying. *The population moves chunks of dirt four times their own body weight.*

Researchers revealed an astounding metropolis of highways, chambers, and ventilated tunnels, Mr. Williams's voice continues in my rattled head. *The ants moved forty tons of soil by doing millions of trips to the surface.*

"Forty tons," I tell Ana.

"Hudson." She slaps my face lightly, shakes me by the shoulders. Her face is contorted and smeared with tears. "Hudson, the ceiling has collapsed. There are people down here, fallen from the community centre, dead and injured. We have to help."

"Is Hudson okay?" Erin's pale face leans into view. "Are you okay, Ana?"

I force my mouth to open, but my tongue is so dry it won't move. My ears feel full of cotton, but I heard Ana and Erin, so I'm not totally deaf. Wait! Ana? Erin? It's coming back to me. Nettle Cave and T-Rex!

I struggle to a sitting position and look at a bowl of blue sky high above. Just over one and a half storeys up to ground level, like the balloon told us. Then, from the rubble around me, I see the wreckage of the community centre and the bodies and hear the groaning, screaming, hollering, and sobbing. It's muted by my messed-up ears but terrifying nevertheless.

Nooo! Not the community centre.

Ana and Erin grab my hands and pull me fully upright. I wince from bruises and cuts on my back, and feel like I've been in a fight that the other guy won, but—

"You okay?" I ask.

"Yeah," Ana whispers, trying to stifle sobs. "We'll get rescued fast, right?" She's looking up at the sky.

"Uh huh. You okay, Erin?"

Erin gives me a trembling thumbs-up.

"Jett and Mica? Wonder if they got out in time. If so, they're probably on their way to the hospital now," I mumble aloud.

We all look out on an immense mess of rocks and rubble, arms and legs protruding into the dust-choked air. There are also unmoving heaps I dare not look at. And faces, some with eyes open, some with eyes closed—all people I recognize. I know I need to move, but my body is frozen in shock. Only my mind works, thoughts flitting through: It's only one and a half storeys. Not like the Big One. Many who fell will survive. I need to help.

"Triage," I shout, my brain fog clearing as I calculate there's something like two dozen people down here. I'm trying to remember instructions from an advanced first-aid class I once took. And I reassure myself that Mom's not here. She'd have been home with Dad. But she'll be crazy worried about me when she figures out what happened.

"What should we do, Hudson?" Erin asks. "And does anyone see my parents?"

"We're going to herd anyone who's alive and able into the centre of the cave. It's the safest place to be, given that debris is going to keep falling down the sides. They need to group tightly, like a football huddle."

"Won't someone start a rescue operation from up top?" Ana asks, wringing her hands.

"It's super unstable at the edges, so they can't just lower ropes. They'll commandeer a crane with an angled rope if we're lucky, but we can't wait for that."

I stare at the Roman amphitheatre-like "statue nooks" in the far wall. "If there are too many people for a safe centre-huddle, drag the injured into those cavities in the walls. Dirt and rock-slides may pour down in front of their faces, but not on them.

"Then start a lineup for Serpent's Squeeze and organize groups of three: two able-bodied carrying one wounded. Dig out what you've got for first-aid supplies and get busy. Erin, are you up to leading those who are okay—and will fit—through Serpent? Don and Dirk have probably gone up to the street to call 911, and they'll guide paramedics through T-Rex and the Serpent into here soon, but we have to get as many people out as we can in the meantime. This place is way unstable."

"Got it," Erin says firmly, marching to the middle of the

disaster zone, checking pulses on the way, stepping gingerly over some bodies, and losing no time in directing those who can move to the centre.

"Where's Dad?" comes Ana's voice. "Has anyone seen my father down here?"

I grip her shoulders and push her away gently. "We need your help, Ana. If he's down here, we'll find him. But you need to help us triage everyone who fell."

Soon the anthill is swarming, some victims helping drag rocks off shouting or whimpering victims, some lining up for Serpent's Squeeze. Though no one has started down it yet.

The population continuously moves chunks of dirt four times their own body weight.

"If ants can do it, so can we," I mutter, prompting a worried look from Ana. Our growing number of helpers, the fallen but still able-bodied, pull some of the incapacitated into the pockets of rock I'd imagined were statue holders. Dazed-looking people, all of whom I know—Coach Barnes, old Mr. Smith, tiny Mrs. Lopez, three members of the Taylor family, Buzz and Avi from my class, Chi Nyugen clutching her screeching toddler—defer to us as if our helmets and lights give us god-like status.

"Hudson!" a helmeted someone shouts as he crawls out of the Serpent's mouth. Tied onto his ankle and emerging with him like bows on a kite's tail are half a dozen first-aid kits and a roll of cloth that resembles slings. The pudgy figure resembles Santa Claus squeezing up a too-tight chimney, accomplishing the feat due to sheer determination and because he's an old pro. Mica's dad! Of course. He's the only other person besides Dad who'd know this route. A rusty caver is still a caver, and he knew what we needed.

"I stepped out of the community centre for a smoke," he explains breathlessly, wiping sweat off his forehead, "and, and—Mica's on his way to the hospital but he insisted I—Well, I'm here."

"Thank you, Mr. Brown," I say, flushed with gratitude. "That was the luckiest smoke ever."

"Agreed," he says grimly and starts untying his supplies and making rounds, offering first-aid kits to any able-bodied survivors willing to help others.

"Those will save a few lives," I say to Ana.

By now, a few would-be helpers from above are tossing ropes and supplies to us. A rumble and tremor halt all activity for a moment. Dirt pours down the sides like sheets of water from Ribbon Falls.

"We need to move people faster!" I shout.

"What can I do?" says a deep voice behind me.

I swing around. "Mr. Williams! You're okay!" I barely stop myself from throwing my arms around him.

"I'm alive," he corrects me, his suit and tie filthy, ragged, and torn, bloody scratches on his face, left arm cradling the limp right. "We do need to move people faster. There's more than one exit out of here, you know." He points to the boulder in front of Firehose Funnel. "I'm going to recruit anyone not too badly hurt to unblock it."

I watch a team form under his coaching. It's treacherous work and triggers a downpour of more debris they need to duck, but a while later, as I look up from bandaging a badly bleeding woman, relief fills me at the sound of a crunch. That's the boulder moving aside, just enough to allow bodies to slip around it.

"Wait!" I shout, before anyone can escape to the unknown corridors between Nettle and Aladdin I. Mr. Williams pauses as

I sprint over and hand him Dad's map. "It goes through places marked Mica's Cave, Aladdin II, and Aladdin I, but don't do any false exits or you'll end up caught in a deadly maze."

Mica's Cave, I found out from Dad's map, had an easy way out around that near-fatal sump.

"Interesting," Mr. Williams says with arched eyebrow, examining the map. "I'll lead a party out with this, get myself a helmet up top, then escort emergency crews in."

"Mr. Williams? I thought you didn't cave."

He shrugs. "I don't. I just map and test water from entrances and exits—or surgences and resurgences, as you underground folk call them. I tried to keep the water from becoming further contaminated by blocking the openings with wire."

"That was you?"

"Of course."

"You put us in danger! We could have been trapped!"

"I… I didn't realize you…"

"All you need to know now is that Dad's map shows the exits between here and Aladdin. Go!"

"Thank you, Hudson." He grips my shoulder, then starts waving survivors through the newly unblocked Firehose Tunnel exit.

"Dad!" someone screams, and I turn to see Ana stooped over a still figure.

By the time I reach her, she has already felt for a pulse on a severely mangled wrist. She collapses when she doesn't get one. I step in, feel a weak beat on his inner neck, place my ear over his mouth—breathless as a dead-end cave—and start cardiopulmonary resuscitation. "One and two and—"

He groans and twists his head sideways to vomit all over his dark, three-piece suit.

"Dad! Dad!" Ana is wailing, tears falling. As she leans over him again, I spy a piece of paper sticking out of her shorts pocket. Dad's map. Stolen from Mica while he lay injured, I calculate, since the only other copy is mine, now in Mr. Williams's hands.

I snatch it back, stare at her, and back away to tend to others. My gut is tight and hurting from more than the wounds on my back now. Thoughts crowd in. Dots start to connect. I push them away as I move from victim to victim, answer questions, and give advice to brave volunteers. Soon we all look up to watch a crane's carefully tilted rescue rope lower downward. Over the next hour it delivers oxygen tanks, stretchers, Search and Rescue cavers, and other emergency responders who circulate among us.

At some point, swaying like I'm about to collapse, I stop to survey the room. Lineups for the two exits have waned to nothing. Slings with severely injured people keep riding up on the crane's power. The statue cubbyholes, some with streaks of blood, are now emptied.

"Son, you need to leave. This place isn't safe, professionals have taken over, and we're wrapping up," says a guy in a helmet, coveralls, and safety vest. "Thank you for your help. You look able to walk out. Wait a few moments and I'll get you a guide."

"Thanks, but I know the way," I say, stumbling toward Serpent Squeeze reassuring the final four survivors waiting for someone to lead them out. The irony that I've achieved my dream—guiding non-cavers through the Door from Castle to Dungeon—is not lost on me. I just wish it hadn't come at such a horrifying price.

CHAPTER TWENTY-NINE

Mom, Dad, and I file out of the church memorial service holding hands. Around us are long faces and whispered well-wishes being exchanged amongst fellow parishioners, some of whom have been through not only this service but have attended the other three as well.

Even so, four deaths out of the twenty-eight who fell the day the community centre caved in was pretty minimal, I remind myself. Some people are still in the hospital, and then there are the rest of us, who have both visible and invisible scars. I wave at the grief counsellor who has been working with all of us in the past month since the disaster. Kind and helpful as she is, my nightmares have diminished only a little. Now I understand Dad's trauma better, even though the Big One was so much worse and so long ago.

Downhill, yellow tape flaps in the breeze around the footprint of the former community centre. What was left of it is now pulled down, and big machines have been filling the sinkhole—filling Nettle Cave—but they stand idle for today. I avert my eyes from where I know Firehose Tunnel and Serpent Squeeze exist beneath the rubble.

I assume we're headed home when Dad steers us toward the memorial garden. We step onto the grounds gingerly, respectfully, Dad and I knowing all too well what lies seven storeys beneath our feet. He sits down on a concrete bench, so Mom and I follow suit.

"If not for you," he says, looking at me, "so many more would have died. Always remember that."

I heave a sigh and shrug.

"We were frantic, both of us," Mom says. "Those were the most horrifying hours of our lives, you being one of the missing. But we're proud of you, Hudson. And so very thankful you came out of it relatively unscathed."

"I should never have given you the combination for the safe—" Dad begins.

"Yes, you should have. You did exactly the right thing, Dad. It was your maps that kept casualties low, allowed people to escape. The whole town knows that. You heard the tribute to you at the service."

"The service was important," Mom says soberly. "All of Tass is still in mourning."

"Like last time," Dad says.

"Can you talk about it?" I ask.

He takes a few moments to gather himself as he stares at his seldom-worn shiny black shoes. "I slipped out of church that day. I was sixteen, my mother was home with the flu, and I didn't feel like sitting through a service that day. I told my dad I'd be right back but wandered down to the school, spotted an abandoned basketball, and was shooting hoops, all on my own, when the ground shook. Shook so hard it was like the world was coming to an end." He breathes heavily. Mom slips an arm around him.

"I saw the church go down like a ship would sink, only ten times faster, the steeple disappearing last. There was so much dust in the air that I dropped the basketball and ran as fast as I could, first away from the disaster and then toward it to help, gasping for breath and trying to process the thing.

"The firehall bell started clanging, and a crowd gathered around the hole. People's mouths were hanging open. People were screaming. Firefighters were shouting to get people back from the edge. Just like earlier this year, when Pool Dome went."

Mom strokes Dad's back. "The parking-lot collapse brought back your nightmares," she says quietly.

"I'd never totally gotten rid of them."

Silence returns for a moment.

"Volunteers gathered up ropes and a crane arrived, and emergency crews got lowered down. They came up grave faced. I kept yelling for Dad and running around the hole frantically till a neighbour led me home. Mom was a mess, and I knew God was punishing me for sneaking out of church, and—"

"Shh," Mom says.

"There were reporters and helicopters and wailing and chaos and—" He shakes his head and covers his eyes with his palms. "The next few years were awful, but not just for me. Everyone had lost someone, and no bodies were ever recovered. Lucas was my best friend at the time. We were already cavers. Dad had taught us. Our escape from the tragedy was to spend hours underground, finding new passages, making maps. Of course, we never went near the old church site. We wouldn't even step into this memorial garden. The memories were too awful, the pain too deep. But it was only a matter of time, I suppose, before our routes edged closer—"

He rubs his face and studies us as if uncertain we want to hear more.

"Keep going, Dad, please," I say softly.

"We were young men by then, proud of our skills, dreaming of finding a cave that would make us famous."

"You wanted to be famous?" I ask, smiling.

"Lucas wanted to be famous. I just liked drawing maps," he says with a wink. "And we didn't know anything about a Rule of Three, although sometimes there were more than the two of us. One summer Tass got an upgrade on its sewer system. It involved a new manhole installation off Main Street."

He goes quiet again. A deer steps into the memorial garden and munches on grass not far away. We all focus on her to tamp down the building tension.

"One night we climbed down the manhole, crawled along until we got blocked by a row of stalactites and stalagmites, and broke one to squeeze through. Forbidden by today's caving code, for sure." He hangs his head. "We dove into a sump and through a hole that got us into a spectacular chamber. We thought we'd discovered a world wonder, but then Lucas's flashlight went off, mine was already weak, and we were in near complete darkness. Batteries didn't last so long in those days.

"Lucas kept fiddling with his, but it wouldn't come back on, and neither of us had a backup. We got good and frightened down there, shivering in the cold and damp. Slowly, it dawned on us where we were, and that's when we started imagining voices and phantoms and all sorts of things, including a clanging bell. We were so totally panicked, we dove back into the sump. Clawing around to pull ourselves through the gap in the wall, we felt the metal of the old church bell that was lodged there and knew instantly what it was. We surfaced and started screaming.

"Lucas shook his flashlight until it blinked on for a few seconds at a time, and we aimed what was left of our beams up and down that wall and saw the bones and screeched so loudly it's a wonder the whole wall didn't collapse on us.

"Somehow, we eventually made it back between the teeth and up to the manhole and out of that place. Lucas was more freaked than me, said he was never going to cave again, and wouldn't even touch the maps we'd made.

"It took me weeks to get him to agree to just one thing: help me block that hole in the wall and scratch a warning sign on it to keep other cavers from following that route. And then seal up the manhole. I told him that until we did that, the disturbed ghosts wouldn't leave us alone. I doubt he believed me, but he ended up joining me on that one last caving stint just to get me off his back."

"And you kept on caving, with other partners, while he never caved again?" I ask.

"Correct. But I never, ever went near that area again, and when you and I started caving together, I vowed to keep you away from the bell, never tell you about it, and never allow you access to the map that showed its existence. Partly for your safety, partly because I couldn't handle talking about it, but mostly to let the spirits, including my dad's, rest in peace."

"I knew you were still haunted," Mom says, "but you've never told me about the bell. I assumed your nightmares and avoidance of this garden were trauma from losing your father in such a horrifying way. You witnessed the worst tragedy the town has ever seen, and at a tender age. I've always known you also suffer from survivor's guilt. I admire how you've dealt with it through counselling, dear, and I appreciate knowing you were trying to protect our son."

"Until I didn't need protecting anymore," I say, squeezing my dad's arm.

"It was awful hiding it from you," Dad says, hanging his head.

"Lying to my own son. Forever steering you and Mica, then Jett, away from where I knew your stupid Door was."

"Our Door ended up saving lives this time around, including Lucas's son," I emphasize.

Dad folds and unfolds his hands. "It was devastating to be bedridden and unable to communicate when you were putting yourself in danger."

"The guilt complex all over again," Mom suggests.

"Then you finally asked the question. Wanted the map. Somehow knew it existed."

"Took all my nerve to ask you, Dad."

"Tore me apart letting you have it, even knowing you'd already found the Bell Wall."

"And now we're back where this conversation started," Mom says. "Acknowledging that the map saved a lot of lives, along with Hudson's bravery and leadership skills."

"I learned from the best," I say. "Thanks for sharing your story finally, Dad."

CHAPTER THIRTY

"The picnic table is free," I say as Ana and I reach Tass Gas. "Let's sit down for a minute."

"Why? Won't we be late for the movie?" Ana asks. She has been hard to track down in the month since the disaster, and seemed less than enthused when I finally insisted we meet for this, our supposed first date, which is really about me getting answers.

"How's your dad?" I begin.

"He'll live, thanks to you, but he won't be working for months. We're moving to Campbell River so his sister, my Aunt Kate, can look after us."

"That's good," I say, not sorry she's leaving town. "Gets you out of his hole, like you wanted all along."

She starts to protest, but instead ends up studying the thin straps of her red sandals.

"You owe me some honest answers, agreed?"

She gives a small nod.

"Why did you want Dad's and my maps so badly?"

She takes a deep breath. "To overlay them with Dad's geology maps. Caving maps reveal where limestone is. Geology maps show definitive lines of impervious rock. Between the two, it's possible to identify 'contact points.' In this region, especially up in the bluffs above town, that means granite intrusions, which may contain deposits of gold."

It's starting to become clear. "Your dad is a prospector."

"He's a geologist, a very good one, and smart geologists make good prospectors. He's also good at administration. That's how he managed to get the TT job, which allowed us to explore this area for contact points. It would have been so much easier if you and I had cooperated early on. Dad wanted to set up a gold claim, get rich, send me to a good university, have great vacations, and all that. Nothing wrong with dreaming, Hudson Greer."

I ignore that and force myself to say the next bit. "You were pretty uncommunicative to start with. Then it suddenly seemed like you were into me. But that was never the case, was it?"

She hangs her head. "Dad told me to wheedle the maps out of you any way I could. You were so—"

"Easy to play," I say, "which you're clearly used to, just like you're good at using people. You get that from your dad, I guess." She flinches, and I'm glad. "I smartened up when I realized you'd lifted my father's map off Mica as he lay there in Nettle Cave kneecapped and in severe pain. Only a jerk would even think of doing that," I say bitterly. "You were totally taking advantage of the situation because you had only one goal in mind."

"Yeah, I know, that was nasty," she admits.

"Did you plant Trog by the cave entrance to divert me from the dye test? How was that going to help your cause?"

"No, I didn't! He's scared of thunder and lightning and ran away."

"Good thing he fell down the hole with me, or you wouldn't have bothered setting up that rescue, would you?"

"Hudson, you're twisting everything to make me sound really evil. I was trying to help my dad, yes. It's the whole reason we were in Tass. I played you at first, sure. Then, when I saw Nettle Cave and understood what was going on and what you were trying to do, I wanted to help. I wanted to cave again, and I knew Dad didn't get what was going on. I started liking Tass about then too, believe it or not, and wanted to stay here. Dad thought I'd lost my mind. Plus, Hudson, I was into you by then. Not that I expect you to believe me," she adds, sounding miserable. "You could say I fell for you when you and Trog fell down that muddy slide together. And then you and your friends were willing to risk your own lives to help the community. Which you did, even if it turned out to be too late to save everyone, thanks to my dad.

"No one at TT knew you were underground when they assigned drivers to fill in those surgences and resurgences," she emphasizes, trying to take my hands in hers. I pull mine free. "Ironically, there were TT guys trailing Mr. Williams and his barbed-wire activities, because it showed them where to in-fill. They just wanted to squelch the town's reputation for sinkholes so they could get on with their tree-felling, which after all supports this community—"

"And TT's profits," I say sternly. "They also hoped it would discourage local cavers from gathering information that might dent the company's reputation."

"That's true too." Her eyes hold mine.

That should send a spark through me, but it doesn't. I feel sadness, tiredness. Almost every time we were together before the Community Centre sinkhole, she was manipulating me.

Not like Erin, who's smart, honest, and a stick of dynamite. Cute too. Our being into each other feels totally natural lately. Hey, I'll have to tell Mica that Dynamite's a good nickname for Erin. And that "Huds" works better than Celery Stick, Chopstick, Toothpick, Twig, Troll, Shrimp, and Runt. Not that I need to anymore, because these days my friend gives the death glare to anyone who makes fun of my size. He has also warmed up to Erin, and not just because she wrote such a great article on Tass's caves and geology. It was for the *Tass High School Gazette*, but a regional paper reprinted it and offered her a journalism internship when she finishes high school. Nowadays, Mica teases me about Erin's face lighting up when I'm around—and me blushing when she comes into a room.

"Ana?" I say, as she sits hunched with her hands squeezed between her knees.

"Yeah?"

"I wish you luck in Campbell River, and I hope your dad gets well."

"I appreciate that, Hudson. Will you keep caving? Still hoping to be a professional cave guide after school?"

I grin. "Remember how my favourite part of caving was naming new spaces?"

She smiles warmly. "Yeah."

"Well, I might get a job as marketing manager. For a local beer company."

"Huh?"

"Mr. Williams is starting a beer brewing business. He has a water lease in progress. He claims the pH levels of the water around Tass match the Bass Beer standard set by Burton on Trent."

"Wherever that is." Ana grins, then frowns. "But he was the one bolting barbed wire on cave entrances and exits."

"Yup, to discourage us from exploring, to keep the water in this region pure. He also pretended he was interested in hot springs to get leads on surgences."

"Well, working for him would allow you to stay in your beloved Tass and keep exploring underground labyrinths without sharing all those spaces with the public's wannabe cavers."

"Exactly. And allow us to keep certain places sealed out of respect for history. I've already amped up my social media, 'Trog's Blog.' Okay that I borrowed your dog's name?"

"Feel free." She laughs.

"My blog informs people about the link between limestone caves, aqueducts, and the importance of a water's pH in beer."

"Tass: World-famous water," she imagines the re-worded welcome sign. "Population: purely refreshed."

I smile. "Hey, I've already proposed a name for the beer company: "Grotto Gold.""

"Hmm. Not quite," she says, looking pained.

"Tass Blast? Reap the Deep? Grotto Lotto? Purely Underground?"

She giggles. "Keep working on it, Huds."

"You know I will."

CHAPTER THIRTY-ONE

Three months later

It's dark as a dungeon ahead, and our hands and knees are throbbing from hours spent in the glorious chamber we've discovered just off Aladdin II. In other words, I as leader, plus Jett, Mica, and Mica's dad, are happy as hungry bats hovering over a mosquito pond.

Yes, we all have moments of panic these days, given what we've been through, but we're all still getting counselling and pushing past that now.

Dad has mostly recovered, gotten his job back (as did Mom), and has even been on two short caving forays, with his doctor's permission.

"Mind the daddy longlegs," Mr. Brown says.

"We don't mind them," I kid back.

Mica's dad has ditched politics to return to real estate and is making an admirable effort to spend more time with his family, even doing Monopoly nights with *our* family—boring. He's also on a fitness kick that helps with his slow transition back into caving. He was on both of my dad's brief trial caving runs, encouraging and supporting him like some kind of coach. Who'd have thought that would ever happen?

"Hey D-squared and Erin!" Jett shouts up the cave entrance to our above-ground crew. "We need more rope!"

"Roger that," Erin singsongs, tossing down another coil.

"Stop calling us D-squared," Dirk says.

"Okay, Dirkster and Donster," Jett teases.

My respect for Jett has grown tenfold in recent months, given he has honed his caving skills and ramped up his confidence. Not only is he a valued member of our team, but his presence gives Dad and Mr. Brown particular reassurance. Why? Because after being hailed as a hero for hauling an injured Mica out that day, Jett started taking advanced first-aid lessons that he hopes to leverage into a job when he graduates. Given how nervous both Dad and Mr. Brown are till they're fully back up to speed (do old guys ever fully get back up to speed?), they like the notion of having a sort-of medic around.

"Enough rope! Stop!" Mica calls up to our surface crew.

"Okay," Erin shouts back cheerfully.

Mica has a stiff knee, but it doesn't slow him down much as he scoots through passages with our newly expanded contingent of underground explorers. He was the one who discovered this beauty, the prize of the decade, off an Aladdin II spur. Even Dad and Mr. Brown had never found it.

"Have you decided what you're calling this chamber of wonders?" Don asks as he descends to our level, manhandling a wheelbarrow down the steep incline. Behind him, Dirk struggles with a water jug, and Erin is peering around their shoulders in her new caving getup.

"Mica gets that honour," I say magnanimously.

"I get the honour, but I'm going with Hudson's suggestion," says Mica, spreading small gravel on the path we've established through this sanctuary.

"And?" Erin asks impatiently, casting her helmet light around the chandelier-like stalactites, stalagmites, soda straws, columns, draperies, bacon strips, and rimstone dams. Yes, this one has it all. Cave pearls and helictites too. It's a perfect demo cave, a textbook example of cave formations.

"The Keep," Mica and I announce together.

"That's dumb. What does it even mean?" Dirk frowns.

"The definition of a 'keep,'" I enlighten him, "is the innermost, strongest structure of a medieval castle."

"I love it!" Erin arranges the rope she threw down earlier between red plastic traffic cones to mark off the tour path, while Mica strings battery-powered twinkle lights around the chamber. "And the tourists will love this place! When do guided tours begin and how much will they cost?"

"Free for Tass citizens the first week," I reply.

"To promote mapmaking," Dad says, appearing at the entrance and grinning big at me.

I smile back warmly. It's so amazing that he has his voice back, though it required some speech therapy.

"I'm mixing," says Don, splitting open the bag of concrete powder mix that sits in the wheelbarrow beside piles of sand and gravel, then waiting for Dirk to pour the right amount of water into the concoction. Dirk produces a trowel, works the solution, and slops the wet cement into wood forms that Mr. Brown has made for the steps up to the entrance.

I shiver as I recall Mr. Toop doing the same, much less competently, to block access to the manhole that night.

Dirk finishes the job like he's icing a cake.

"Pretty smooth, Dirk," I say. "Looks professional."

"Thanks," he replies, head cocked.

I'm super pleased that regional Parks Canada bureaucrats gave preliminary approval for this section of cave to go public. We argued that it would help the community heal. Many townspeople agreed.

"The lights and ropes also look great, Erin and Mica," I add. "Especially the spotlight you put in that floor nook, which perfectly backlights the popcorn, soda straws, and bacon strips." In this location the soda straws are almost as long as I am tall. Popcorn are small bundles of flowstone that make me want to melt butter and watch a movie. Honestly, though, they're kind of a geologic miracle, given that it takes water seeping through limestone walls and leaving deposits that react with carbon dioxide and minerals to form these multi-headed bubbles.

"This place is as good as Kartchner Caverns or Little Caves, right, Dad?"

"Ha!" he says with a wink.

"Hello, work crew!" comes a woman's voice from up top. It's Mom, with Mica's mom.

"Come on down, as long as you sidestep the wet concrete," Mr. Brown says.

Mom in her jeans and hiking boots, Mrs. Brown in a skirt and low-heeled sandals, and Dad moving slowly but steadily, pick their way through the entryway till they're standing in the Keep.

"Oh my!" Mrs. Brown says, her hand over her mouth. "All this, right here in Tass! And just a short stroll from daylight! Wait till we post photos on the tourist website!"

"It's as magnificent as you described it," Mom says, setting down a picnic basket full of sandwiches and home-baked things she and Mrs. Brown have concocted. "And that's saying something." She wraps her arms around Dad and me, and we have a family hug, prompting Erin to wink at me.

"Got your cave-guide speech ready, boys?" Mr. Brown asks.

"Of course," I reply. "Mr. Williams helped us with it. He's also helping me prepare for the regional science fair next month, which is pretty generous considering how much time his business start-up needs."

"He's a good man," Mr. Brown says.

"He is," Dad agrees.

"Win the science fair and it'll be great publicity for our caving tour," Mica says.

"You never know."

"So, commence with your speech then," Mrs. Brown suggests.

"Karst landscapes are areas where water erodes underground limestone, producing a complex and fragile environment," I begin.

"Such areas cover twenty percent of the land surface in North America, and are key to clean drinking water," Mica puts in.

"Uh-uh," Dad interrupts, shaking his head and wagging a finger.

"Too boring? We need to kick off with local history and cave formation science?" I ask. "Talk about the fragile environment?"

"No," Dad says, "we need to roll out this picnic before you roll out your charming tour script."

"I second that," says Mom.

Ha! Charming tour script?

"Have a seat, ladies," I say, gesturing to two camping chairs and eyeing the contents of the picnic basket as they lift its lid. We cavers group ourselves at the women's feet as they lift out sandwich buns, drinks, muffins, and more.

Dirk looks at Mr. Brown and Dad. "All these years, you two old guys secretly knew where the Door was that we guys were fighting each other to find?"

"We did," Mr. Brown answers soberly with a glance at Dad.

"Dad, I understand why you kept some of your master maps locked up, secret even from me," I say, "but why did you keep on caving at all? Why were you always excited to map when you were with us, even though you'd already mapped those places?"

"New technology and methods," he says, "make better maps. And I was spending quality time with my son." He winks.

"So, you were improving your maps while revisiting places you let us think we were discovering."

"I was leading, teaching, and doing what I love," he says.

I eye surrounding cave formations, wanting to reach out and touch their beauty but respecting their fragility. I fast-forward in time to picture Mica and me leading groups of wide-eyed citizens into the magical corridors of science. Leading, teaching, personally thriving, and heedless—well, almost heedless—of fame. Yes, our tours will get written up and vacationers will flock here, some even asking for Mica and me by name. But even as I reach into the picnic basket and lock loving eyes with Dad, I'm mentally editing the guide script to add more pizazz, more show of passion for what we truly love.

ACKNOWLEDGMENTS

I'm indebted beyond words to Rick Cole, Vancouver Island caving Search and Rescue guy, who spent hours helping me with plotting and writing, and who shared an armload of binders and manuals. He has extraordinary patience and knowledge, and passion for the sport. That said, any errors are mine alone.

I was originally inspired both by a Kartchner Caverns tour in Arizona and time spent wriggling through Upana caves near Tahsis, B.C., on which Tass is based. My husband was horrified when I climbed down into Devil's Bath sinkhole, but both of us were charmed by Tahsis and its welcome sign: "Population: more or less." (Meanwhile, a local pub has signs reading, "Beer is free tomorrow." "Drinking town with a fishing problem." "Shut up and fish.")

The town's website states that "Tahsis is without a doubt Canada's ecotourism caving mecca! Cavers from all over the world come to explore the more than fifty kilometres of passages found so far in the mountains around town."

Apologies to Tahsis residents for fictionalizing many of the town's aspects and features.

I was obviously intrigued by Rick's comment that a church really was swallowed by a sinkhole in that region many years ago (but not with anyone inside).

I was sobered by PBS's Nova documentary, *Sinkholes: Buried Alive*. I gained valuable perspective from James M. Tabor's

Blind Descent, Andy Sparrow's *The Complete Caving Manual*, and Paul Burger's *Cave Exploring*. I also drew upon information in Kurt Repanshek's *National Parks Traveler* article, "Two Caves That May Have a Connection?" (Jewel and Wind Caves, South Dakota); "Wind Pressure in Caves" by allsensors.com; Tasmanian geomorphologist Kevin Kiernan's "Forest Sinkhole Manual" (Forest Practices Board, Tasmania); and "How to Survive an Opening Sinkhole" by whatifshow.com.

Last but definitely not least, thanks to all the team at Yellow Dog, especially Catharina de Bakker, Anita Daher, Keith Cadieux, and Mel Marginet. Also, thanks to agent Amy Tompkins, my valued friend and editor Allyson Latta, my husband Steve, and teen editors Jett Samson, Bella Nelstrop, and Juliet King.